From the Viewpoint
of a Starling

FROM THE VIEWPOINT OF A STARLING

A. C. VERNON

First published in 2013 by Bunty Bussell Books

Bunty Bussell Books
11 Bath Road
Ashcott
Somerset TA7 9QS

ISBN 978-0-957561 7-0-0

Cover design by
Florian Zumfelde

British Library Cataloguing in Publication Data.
A catalogue record for this book is available from the British Library.

Typeset in Palatino by Troubador Publishing Ltd
Printed and bound in the UK by TJ International, Padstow, Cornwall

www.buntybussell.com

To rock and roll, and small towns everywhere.

1

The Dockside Wall

Building the wall was hard; for the laying of the stone and mortar was a skill requiring not only a knowledge of angles, but also a steady hand and tough skin.

The men who built the wall all those years ago, were local men to Backton. They'd been born here, grown up here, learnt their trade here, and so there was a degree of patriotic pride when they worked on the wall down by the dock. And they worked hard. They applied their knowledge thoughtfully, mixed the mortar smoothly, chiselled the stone evenly, laid the bricks precisely. When the chisel slipped and cut their hands, it was a mark of camaraderie and unity, the blood seeping into the mortar like a brotherly kind of seal. The blood was also an awareness of the future, although the men never spoke about that. It was an awareness of giving your time and your art and your pain to protect others, to keep them safe from the riverbank in order to live their lives.

As they mixed and chiselled and chipped and bled, the men would sing. Sometimes the songs were low and soft: sad ballads of misplaced love. Other times, the songs were loud and lusty: drinking songs that resounded off the stone in their hands and echoed away upstream. And as they sung, the men saw the fish in the water. They saw the rushes and mallow on the riverbank, and once they saw a Trumpeter swan. This was before the Industrial Revolution, when their grandsons built the factories and the chimneys. It was before the Victorian terraces and the laying of the roads, and well before the housing plans and sub-suburban existence.

So now in Backton Dock, the fish have gone from the water, and the rushes and mallow are hard scrub-grass. In Pound Street, off the main town, the Victorian terraces crumble together. At the junctions, the traffic queues as ever, jamming and bottlenecking, and the rubbish piles up on the pavements. There is a Sainsbury's store here, an Asda, an Aldi, a Lidl, a Somerfield somewhere, no Waitrose, a Tesco (built on the site of a public park), a soon-to-be Morrisons, and an Iceland. M&S shut down years ago.

And how many pubs are here?

More than sufficient.

And how many gift shops?

Just one – new, bright, light and hopeful, sprinkled with pink scented candles and soaps.

Down by the river, mid-town, where the water shifts as thick as cement, rots Backton Dock and its wall. The men who built it died, a long, long time ago.

2

Diary – My Life Continues

Wednesday.
It's only Wednesday.
It's neither one thing nor the other.
God it drags, this life.

Anyway.

I wake up early. I know it's early: there's light from somewhere. Not from the sunshine, more a grey light from the clouds. It's there, where the curtains don't meet in the middle, though I pull them hard each time.

If there was a hill beyond the curtains, outside beyond the house, a hill that led from the dirty street, right up to the peak lost in the grey light of the clouds, I might walk it. Right up to the peak and the edge of the clouds. Only there's not. There are other houses like this one, and beyond those, other houses, and the roads with the waste paper flying in the air.

Anyway.
Wednesday.
It's only Wednesday.

I wake up early, say "No" to personal hygiene, and just throw on the clothes that scatter the floor: the trousers, shirt and usual purple tie. I know this sounds repulsive and I totally agree – it is, yet I've learnt it's not only acceptable, but the regular staff practice: no point washing before 'That Place' – the kids' Lynx-stink will hide the smell.

I pick up the usual briefcase, the usual lesson plans, the usual I.D. badge and a pile of posters – *that* is my main aim: early in the grey light, free publicity, stick the posters up quickly, covertly, all over, no messing.

So when I'm out on the doorstep, I see him, with his brightly polished shoes and his neatly combed hair, my landlord. He's the only person in the street who would have made such an attempt at personal grooming at this early hour (or any hour) – my landlord. And lord he certainly is, make no mistake about that, presiding over this miserable back-to-back as if it were Castle Howard. In Aran's head, his two lodgers are the tourists who hang about, ready to pinch the family stainless steel from the plastic cutlery tray: we need to be followed and kept in check at every available point.

So when I'm out on the doorstep, just leaving for the day (normally and innocently and, I think, within the terms of the law), I see him. Aran. He's there already, up already. Does he sleep? If he does, it's standing up, with open eyes watching. I've often wondered how old he is. I don't actually know (I've never asked and he's never said), but I bet he looks older than he is, and he looks about 50. It must be the strain of constant surveillance that pinches his pointed face.

And now it's 7am and he's up already, out in the front yard, with the snapped trellis and the cat dirt, watching me on his peripheral vision and snipping at the pale patch of lawn with an old pair of nail scissors.

I have a dream of a tiny thatched cottage, requiring no references, no deposit, on my own, rent-free.

Five minutes later, Aran left behind in the yard and my dreams of a tiny thatched cottage over, I'm jackhammering the staple-gun into town billboards. I make an artistic arrangement in a skewed design, posters leaning left, overlapping, no parallels, like a local Picasso and It. Looks. Good! I also 'do' the bus shelters, a couple of traffic lights, a municipal skip, and the developer's sign on the Morrisons site. All completed before the rush of the morning. Well in time to pull in the punters. So that's all right.

    With just half an hour left before hell, I park by a boarded shop, then lean over the town bridge and watch the bore below as it curls along the dockside wall. The wall is foundering to the river and the darkening wave. The wave trails silt in its wake and slaps against the upturned frame of a bike.

God it drags, this life.

Anyway.

    'That Place'? Long and tedious, so I'll be quick and quicker.

    As soon as I step in the front corridor, there are two people in my path: firstly, Shania (hair, heels, hollering) and secondly, Linda Hart (spiky vice-head). The conversations run as follows:

    Shania; "Oi! Mr Price! Got yer purple ponce-tie on then?!"

The other girls, her devilish team of acolytes, smother their laughter.

Shania; "Oi! Mr Price! We saw yer posters."

Me (nervously); "Did you?…Well done."

Shania (seductively); "Yeah, and we be really lookin' forward to it."

The acolytes murmur in approval.

Me (panicking); "What?!… You? …You can't. It's over 18s. You can't."

There's a general rumbling of disagreement.

Then Shania (triumphantly and slightly vindictively); "Oh yeah we can. My uncle works be'ind bar so we be definitely comin'."

They teeter off down the corridor and I'm left with the sudden and all-consuming fear that my first gig in years is not going to run as smoothly as I'd initially planned.

The second conversation starts with a snappy yap in my ear:

"Martin!" (That'll be Linda.) "Martin! … Oh… I see you're wearing your purple tie … *again*."

Honestly!

"I need you to swap period five with Norman, so you'll be covering Year Ten detentions instead."

Me (panicking *again*); "What?!"

Linda (joyfully); "Thank you *so* much."

And that's what I did – relinquished my only free lesson to nanny a livid gang of teenagers, whilst Norman had a little quiet time elsewhere, and the teenagers punched the tables.

Let's forget the rest.

3.30.
Thank God.

If there was a hill beyond the curtains, that led from the dirty street, right up to the peak and the edge of the clouds, I might walk it.

3

THE COMMUNITY CLUB

Down a side street, around a canine-shitted corner, past some corporate wheelie-bins smelling of stale milk, and into the cob-walled club.

Here is where the community flag flies.

Doggedly. Throughout the last 50 years of district decline.

Doggedly and dog-eared: a stoical statement of neighbourly hope.

Plus there's cider – Rumpley's rough and lush, Somerset variety. £2.50 a pint, £1.50 a half, 80p a quarter (which is surprisingly popular on a Friday night, when the Child Support's paid and the money's tight), but "don't ask for credit, as refusal offends."

Down the broken stone steps, through the front door and the damp passage, to the scuffed, brown lino of the club.

The brown lino dictates the standing/leaning area, where drinks are ordered across the beer-towelled bar from George – large-bellied, low-trousered, 51. Or from Rita – short, kindly, 55, who also prepares the cheese and onion rolls, cling-filmed and displayed in a plastic basket-weave bowl.

And then carpet – the hard, resilient, tiled type, sponge-able, mop-able and occasionally steam-cleanable. It was on this very same carpet that Harry Halibut had his head stoved in with a heavy jar of coins after an argument with Mickey the Moocher, or Mickey the Murderer as he became known. The argument was over the ownership of a pickled egg (also available from the bar) which turned out to be someone else's entirely anyway. The jar of coins was the result of a fund-raising Bingo night in aid of the Community Club yard (a climbing pink rose, some azaleas, two deck chairs, and gravel). So, post egg and jar, the police came, the paramedics came, and Rita had the carpet-tiles steam-cleaned. The stain is not so bad.

The brushed velour sofas are pushed together in the corner, musty and fag-burned from the days when the cigarette smoke hung in the air and no-one stood on the pavement. Uneven legged chairs surround a small uneven stage, and on Saturday nights "Bruce Boonsby with his guitar" sits here, his vinyl-topped bar stool tipping back and forth on the join. When he asks for requests, there are the customary replies: "My fist, your face!" "A pint of Rumpley's!" And once: "Your wife's arse from behind!" (That person went too far and George showed them the white lines in the road.) The songs are always the same – sweetly sung ballads, lilting and soft as the balls on the pool table clatter:

Blanket on the Ground.

The Crystal Chandelier.

Ruby, Don't Take Your Love to Town.

Songs from other times, other places – unseen, unattainable places – but with words that are understood: love, heartbreak: the realities of life.

4

DIARY – MY LIFE ENDS

Friday.

12 noon.

I feel sick.

Nerves – kicking in early. God I hope there's no kicking-in *later*. Might be rough there.

Well, this is it.

Tonight's the night (Neil Young song!).

God I wish *I* were Neil Young.

I busy myself with meaningless tasks: smooth my duvet; straighten my shoes; count the number of Nurofen left in the box. I think of food, but the thought tightens my stomach. I haven't eaten since yesterday. Perhaps I *should* eat. I go downstairs, but Aran is there in the kitchen, ironing. He has no ironing board, so lays a towel on the table instead. On first glance it seems as if he's ironing nothing. And then I see his shoelace – neat, flat, steaming. Aran's face is a picture of smug self-satisfaction.

"Morning," I venture.

Aran stops ironing, and deliberately checks his watch. "Afternoon," he replies, pointedly.

"Yes," I say.

The iron hisses and Aran sighs. "There." He holds up the lace, and his eyes glint and blink at me from behind his glasses. "Now I'm all ready… for tonight."

Oh no.

5.30; "Get a grip!"
6 o'clock; "Get a grip will you!"
6.30; nearly get a grip.

By 7 o'clock I am at the Club, onstage and waiting, fingers poised ready on the first chord. Unfortunately, it is now, as I stand geared up to begin, that I am foolish enough to think in terms of 'reverse psychology': "Fearing the worst means it will turn out fine." It is a positive thought – confidence boosting and relaxing. And then in comes the crowd – all one of them. He is big, pierced and tattooed; the word "Roxy", blue on the back of his shaven head. He is an intimidating sight, bringing my new-found assurance plummeting even lower than before. Without a word, he sits at the bar, nods at me, and George pulls him a quarter pint.

8 o'clock and with a few more Club members staring in my direction, George shouts; "All right then boy, might as well get on with it!"

Might as well.

Over the next hour or so, as George pulls more quarters and the cider soaks in, certain events occur which can only be described as 'lowlights':

First of all: the heckling. I thought there might be a bit, but I was wrong. There's a lot. It's entirely contributed by the 'Roxy

11

tattoo' and is composed of one repeated phrase: "When's the band comin' on? When's the band comin' on? When's the band comin' on?" He shouts it again and again, consistently, loud and thuggish, between songs and during them, and every time it receives a laugh and every time I laugh too, not because I think it's funny, but because I have an obviously desperate desire to get the audience to like me. They don't.

Then there's the jukebox. Seeing as live music is onstage, I thought it might be turned off, but again I was wrong. It's not, and it's proving better entertainment than me. I hear it beneath my chords, and its sound is as repetitive as the heckling, and also between songs and during them: Glenn Campbell, Neil Diamond, Glenn Campbell, Neil Diamond, Glenn Campbell, *The Prodigy?* I joke about it into the mic; "Hey, I've got some great songs here. Who needs the jukebox?" This is answered by the rattle of 20p in the slot, and *Rhinestone Cowboy* ringing out for the fifth time.

When Aran and Taser arrive, I am already unnerved and faltering on the simplest of chords. However, the sight of them unnerves me more and I am virtually unable to play. For a start, it's surprising to see Aran out in public, and surprising to see Taser, the other lodger, awake before 8pm, but the two out together? I miss a D minor. Whilst Aran sits stiffly at the back on a hard, upright chair and observes me with barely-concealed contempt, Taser, sleepy-eyed and really not with it yet, fumbles his way to the bar. To Taser, I'm probably not here, and that's OK by me.

Honestly, things might've turned out all right, the evening might've been salvaged had there not been any further distractions. For I am just beginning to regain composure by managing a basic 'A' major, when there's an unexpected screeching at the door. It's another entrance, as equally unnerving as the last. It's the entrance of Shania with familiars, and their voices cutting like glass shards through my ragged playing. They are squawking; high-pitched, excited parrot squawks of "*There he is! Look! Look! Look Shan, there he is!*" Several of the audience, jolted by the screeching, turn in surprise towards me as if they hadn't yet realised there was actually anyone or anything to look at. Then, in a crackle of nylon static, Shania and friends rush to the front of the stage (empty by the way) and stop right in front of me, and giggle and stare. I have no idea why they stay there: it's not as if there's a pack of people all pushing for a view of the 'stars', but they keep this position the rest of the evening, tottering and tittering, and carbonating their girly effervescence further from miniature bottles hidden in one of their bags.

Of course, with an entrance, you'd expect an exit, possibly from the spectators, but unusually tonight it's from 'the band'. It's Rodney. Rodney is drumming, on his Fisher-Price snare and high-hat beside me. It's just us, a rock 'n' roll duo. However, soon I'm a rock 'n' roll solo, for mid-song he just suddenly stops, stands and says; "Sorry Mart. I can't do this anymore. Wrists are hurting." As he steps down the stage, he announces loudly: "*Too much wanking!*" and leaves, with his drumsticks and a half-empty pint. I am left, mumbling a sort of apology to an uninterested crowd until finally…

The Kiss: lip-sticked and forceful, hard on the mouth, from a woman 'of a certain age'. She staggers up on the stage from somewhere, presses her lips heavily on mine, then pulls my head to her bosom and bellows; "*Ahh, bless 'im. 'Ee did lovely,*

13

poor lad!" She smells of Dubonnet, and I get a round of applause (though not for my musical talent, I suspect).

As she clutches me in a neck-breaking stranglehold, I struggle free to see a gentle-faced, slightly balding man. He is sitting at the bar, watching and smiling, and by his side is an acoustic guitar like mine, and on it is a sticker; "Alicante".

The jukebox continues (now *Achy Breaky Heart*), and I pack up.

My guitar has no stickers, just scratches, and the case is battered from busking on Slovakian street corners sometime in the past. The inside though, is clean and smooth with a comforting scent of wood, and steel strings, and there's a pocket for plectrums. I feel inside for the tatty piece of paper from a cheek-boned girl.

"Oi! Mr Price!" The shrill words jab at my consciousness like a fake fingernail in the eye.

"Oi! Mr Price. That were great." Shania and the covern are standing far too close, their black mascara lashes flapping heavily in my face.

"Oh, right, thank you," I say, slightly stunned by their enthusiasm. I'm also stunned by their proximity, and trying to inch backwards, but Rodney's drum-kit affair prevents me.

"Yeah, *really* great, especially that last bit when Rosie *tongued* you. We nearly pissed ourselves!"

I knock the drum-kit over, and they nearly piss themselves again.

"Never mind," consoles Shania. "My older brother's in a band. Good he is. Singer/guitarist an' that. P'raps he could give you some tips."

14

And they go, pissing themselves harder than ever.

"Well, well, well. Well done. *Well* done indeed." Aran is next, sidling up to me, smarmy and snide. "I never realised I housed a lodger with such ability. Well done indeed." He snuffles to himself in delight. "*Such* ability. And here, of all… *venues*." He gestures in a sweeping arc around the shabby room, to the pints of cider, the stained floor and the cracked jar of coins on the bar.

I must admit, the Community Club is one of the last places I'd expect to see Aran – an abattoir possibly, or a public execution, but not *here*. I imagine him in a uniform, not dissimilar to that of the Third Reich, and I can't help but admire his sheer depth of spite that he is willing to tolerate an evening with the 'people' in order to witness my almost total humiliation. Once more I see the tiny thatched cottage, rent-free etcetera, and for a moment, forget it's a dream.

"Aran," I say. "I'm leaving."

Aran smiles – more than I've ever seen him smile before.

5

BRUCE BOONSBY

When Bruce Boonsby opens his front door and steps inside from the pot-holed pavement of Pound Street, he thinks of his wife. She is here, everywhere, in the air, in the ether; her laugh, her voice so light and soft, her little brown bob, her deep brown eyes. She is here and everywhere and nowhere. Not dead, no, though that would be so much better – cold in the earth and rotting. For his wife Susan, pretty, understanding and timid, had been unfaithful.

Bruce had felt bad wishing she would die, watching her leave with her case, watching her get in the taxi, wishing it would crash. How do you reconcile these thoughts, this situation, with your belief in humanity and God? But there it was. And it was done. And undone – the past 33 years unravelled in a moment.

Bruce's house, once also Susan's house, is now in his name entirely. And when he opens his front door and steps inside, he wishes this fact away; "There is always the possibility she might return; the knock at the door, the key in the lock, the face at the window, and so on. There is always the possibility, the option, the clause to add her name again. What's mine is yours, and so on."

But it's a long way from Alicante.

It had been a surprise, and not in a good way, to realise her infidelity whilst on a package break away – a special offer in the Backton Bugle; "*Discover the delights of this beautiful resort. £400 for one week in a traditional Spanish hotel, including dinner, bed and breakfast, together with en-suite accommodation and the services of an over-attentive waiter.*" Bruce had discovered the delights, all right. Just two days in.

After her prolonged disappearance from a beachside stroll (on the pretext of a migraine), Bruce decided to take his wife some iced bottled water from a drinks stall. In true sit-com style as the lift doors opened, he chanced upon Pedro leaving their room, dishevelled and breathless, but nevertheless, somehow victorious and proud.

The rest of the holiday was spent alone, and the flight home in silence.

Now Bruce felt bad no longer, wishing she were dead, only drained by the passage of events. For time had passed and what remained was a relentless chaos of hope – constantly, against all reason, hope – draining and tiring. So death would have solved that issue: no chances then, no key in the lock with the cold wet earth on her corpse. And the wish for her demise was less violent, arising as it was, not from hate, but instead from the need for relief: no high-speed car crash on the Backton Bypass, a brief, non-specific illness, perhaps, just to quietly take her off.

Maybe she was already dead and all his hoping wasted. But then he'd never know. And so the circle continued, the not knowing fuelling his hope that she would some day, one day, return.

17

Bruce Boonsby opens his front door, steps inside and thinks she's there. His wife. He slowly removes his overalls, grey with the factory grime, then sits in the chair and hopes.

6

DIARY – MY LIFE BEGINS

Rejoice!
At last:
Goodbye 'That Place'.
At last:
There is light.
The Good News;
Go tell it on the mountain:
"Martin Price Music Promotion is here!"

I'm on a sofa. And it's not *my* sofa. This one is dark blue, in a darkened room with a window straight onto the pavement. There is an unfamiliar smell of books and industrial oil. Books are all over – on shelves, on tables, spilling over in piles on the floor. And there's a guitar – an acoustic guitar like mine. And a grimy grey overall on a chair.

Oh God, thank God for Bruce Boonsby. He saved my skin at the Club last night after that 'Aran issue': I gave up my lodgings – had nowhere to go.

I find Bruce outside in his garden – the tiny terrace backyard.

He's taken a rickety kitchen-stool and set it on the crazy paving amongst the geranium pots and the weeds. And he's sitting, just sitting, with a cup of tea.

"Hello lad."

"Thanks Bruce."

"That's all right. Kettle's boiled."

I bring the other rickety stool and we sit companionably. Beyond the brick wall, in the near distance, the sound of the town punctuates the silence, and the bell of St. John's, at odds with the car horns, chimes the hour.

"Right then," says Bruce. "Time I was moving."

I get up as well, but he motions me to stay. "That's all right lad. You needn't go, just because I am."

He goes inside the house and when he re-emerges, he's buttoning up the grey overalls. "Work. Rubber. Shift," he mutters in explanation.

"Rubber?" I say. " I thought it was closing down."

"'Tis. But not yet."

Bloody hell. The Rubber Factory – what a nightmare: on a side street off the main town, by the river and a scrubby, brownfield wilderness. It seems noxious there, or rather the gas emitting from its towering redbrick chimney seems noxious – a strange, toxic mixture of chemical and industry. And now crisis: after a long local history of rubber and job provision, crisis corroding the black heart of Backton in an economic meltdown.

"33 years, me." Bruce looks up at the church spire and pauses… "But not yet, boy."

"That's a long time."

"Yes," he replies sadly. "But there 'tis."

I get a bit awkward at this point and don't know what to say next. It's already an unemployment-waste-bowl of a town. Not many alternatives likely to present themselves to 100 workers out on their backsides. I stare at the dregs of my tea. Bruce however, turns and goes back inside and suddenly I hear him laugh.

"That other lad, who is it...*Aran*?" he snorts from the kitchen. "You're better off out of that. There's another room upstairs, if you need it. For a while."

And just like that, in a few words, Bruce Boonsby saves my skin for a second time.

"Thanks Bruce."

"That's all right."

He appears in the doorway again, clutching a Tupperware box and a green tartan flask. He hesitates.

"Just need to tell you something though."

"OK."

"Last night."

"Yes?"

"Community Club"

"Yes?"

"You were..." he hesitates again. "...Good."

"Thanks."

"To a degree."

"Er...right."

"Near the beginning."

"...Right."

He looks sorry. "You know lad, you have to...pick your audience...and your place; other music, other people, other place? Might work." He goes back in and the front door slams behind him.

Dear, sweet Jesus!

It's as if a ray of light suddenly beamed from the sky. As if a heavenly choir of angels sung out, and the crashing chords from a risible rock opera resounded all around. God, when I die, I will remember at this moment I was happy!

Thanks Bruce.

High Noon

I'm down on the council estate in search of my fortune. I say, "council estate", it's ex-council really. Most of the houses are bought now. Post-war semis and 1960s high-rises, or housing association – rented, sub-rented and squatted. It's on a long, wide, treeless main road with humps and chicanes to slow the boy racers and the increase in infant mortality. Halfway up, a small precinct serves the community, with a Bill Hill betting shop and Super-Buy. Directly opposite, set between American Nails and a Cash Converters, is the pub – The Man in the Moon, a 3-storey, stone-clad block, with its door wide open and its windows boarded. As I say, I'm in search of my fortune.

Anyway, it's busy here: boys on bikes and Rip-Sticks, girls in huddles watching. There are dogs tied up by the shop and some running free and leg-cocking. There is the sensation of broken glass crunching underfoot, and there is noise everywhere; shouting, barking, music, engines. And from somewhere I hear that sound, the sound of a searing guitar and a punchy, dead-beat drum.

Bruce Boonsby, if you're right, this could be the start of something big!

It's not long before I find Shania. I see her across the road. She's by some old lock-up garages – dented silver-grey doors – standing with another girl, both concentrating, focussed on their hands.

After a deep-backed Saxo shoots through the chicane, I cross the road to see that Shania and friend are expertly rolling cigarettes. They look up as I approach, and shout something, but the guitar is loud now and from behind the garage door, the backfill drumbeat immerses their words. Shania boots the door with her foot, the music stops and when the door grates slowly open, the boys inside blink as the glare of sunlight floods the gloom.

Suddenly it's bizarre, like a bizarre scene from *Oliver*: there must be 20 teenagers inside the garage, the skinny, scruffy boys hidden in Fagin's lair. And they've been sitting in the dark, on the floor, on rolled-up hoodies, or on boxes and upturned buckets whilst the band plays – three boys; drum, guitar and bass.

"Why couldn't I hear the bass?" I ask.

"Pissing lead's bust," replies the bassist, a short lad in long baggy shorts and glasses.

"Oi Lofty! It's not the lead that's bust, it's *you*," jibes the guitarist, a taller lad with low-slung jeans and long black hair. "You're shit. You play like a fuckin' ape."

"*You're* shit," retorts Lofty.

This will be my fortune, if they agree: "other music, other people, other place." Get a gig, get a crowd, get a fee, take half.

They agree.

Martin Price Music Promotion is here.

Thanks Bruce.

7

MUDDY BLACKMORE

Muddy Blackmore was not his real name – the lad in the band, the one with the low-slung jeans and long black hair. '*Muddy Blackmore*' was a pseudonym. At least, the '*Muddy*' part was. Muddy Blackmore was a creative musical genius who didn't give a fuck if the volume went to 11, and if you couldn't hear the words. In fact, that was better. And if the notes got lost, well, that was OK too.

When Muddy played guitar, jamming good with Nige and Lofty, something happened; a movement away, a spiriting to another world. Transcendental bullshit and all that, but Muddy was there, away with the gothic/grunge fairies, in a world of light and meaning.

Michael Blackmore, on the other hand, was just a lad in a band: any lad, in any band, in any town. And that was a bit pissy really because this town was nothing more than a deep, dark pit of wasted time. "It's just a construct," Michael thought. "A social construct by local bureaucracy in which people 'like us' are constrained and suppressed. And I'm not gonna friggin' play that game."

So Michael, 18, and a bit annoyed at his lot, picked up his guitar and crafted some species of sound; sometimes melodic, sometimes discordant, but always loud.

It had started in the bedroom a few years ago, on a wide-necked, plastic-stringed Spanish guitar he'd bought for £10 from an advert in the Backton Bugle: "*2nd hand, slightly scratched, needs 3 new tuning pegs.*" This was not, truly speaking, the first guitar though. The first one was bought for £25 (which he'd saved from washing cars). He'd told an older boy at Backton Secondary School that he'd needed a guitar and was willing to pay. Said guitar was duly produced and, in due course, so was a warning from the police, for the guitar turned out to be stolen, from the Backton Secondary School music room. "What a complete durr-brain," thought Michael, "to pay over the odds for one that was nicked from about six feet away." He was excluded for two weeks, lost the money, the guitar, and a ticket to the school gig in which he had also bagged a slot operating the mixing desk. "What a shit!"

The first *legal* guitar, the £10 Spanish, was the start of the long hard rock 'n' roll road. Michael got callouses on his fingers from pressing the plastic strings. It hurt his wrist as his hand stretched around the wide neck. He struggled to reach the chords, and it was a bugger learning to play *and* sing both at the same time. His older brother Steve, with whom he shared the bedroom, complained that the musical output was tedious and tuneless and that the guitar was always in the way of his porn mags. This was all true, so Michael persevered – by keeping the guitar out of the way of *Big Butts, Big Tits*; by varying his scales; and by playing easy pieces Steve might appreciate: *Fulsom Prison, House of the Rising Sun, Stairway to Heaven*, (that last one was a bit difficult actually).

It was, perhaps, not surprising as the guitar took over and

25

he became more accomplished, that school slipped into the background. Michael had never shone at Backton Secondary, very few had. It was the sort of establishment found in every struggling borough – the sort that had missed out on the *Building School's for the Future* plan, and now lay disintegrating to the past. On the Western Distributor Road, within gobbing distance of the magistrates' courts, it was the sort of establishment forced to focus its attention onto the mass of underachieving boys who slumped into its wide economically challenged catchment area. Boys like Michael, who glimmered in an average light, were simply invisible, unseen in the maelstrom of dragging angry, abused meatheads up to a grade 'G'. "Who *is* Michael Blackmore anyway? Which tutor group? Mine?"

With absolutely no application or encouragement, Michael left school with seven GCSEs, including Maths and English, at grade 'C'. A shame probably, and Michael realised too late that somehow he'd been cheated. Brother Steve, about to join the army, watched him as he pummelled his energy into the guitar, playing along to Bob Dylan, in front of the half-length mirror, playing for real, looking authentic.

"You've gotta do something Mike, like a job or something. You can't just stay in here now – school's over. Why don't you go and busk or something. Make some money from it."

After two days spent on the corner of the shopping precinct, receiving 57p, and a Nike trainer in the head, Michael stopped busking and secured a part-time job cleaning the chimney at the Rubber Factory instead. The men there spurred him on, told him he was young and bright and that school had shat on his chances. So he made a late application to Backton's tiny subsidiary college (range of portakabins), with some pre-foetal idea of studying Music Technology and Resistant Materials. However, a week into college, Michael had lost interest in RM and changed to Art (a vague interest in the pop technique of Warhol). This was what the pretty bunnies studied, with their tight-arsed jeans and bleached fringes, so what the hell if he couldn't hack it.

By now, brother Steve was hiding in a sand-trench in Afghanistan, and Michael had the room to himself. Whilst Shania was at school and his Mum was working in one of her four jobs, he skived off Art and tried to sneak a bunny or two back home. But it never worked out: they were from the other side of town, too posh and Michael too skanky.

All the while though: music. And soon the £10 Spanish was not enough – too quiet, too staid, too beautiful. Michael needed more; more sound, more driving, thrashing sound. So, with some remnants of an EMA allowance, together with some cash in hand from the Rubber and a small loan from his Mum's cleaning, he bought his first electric – a Peavey Raptor Plus EXP in trans blue, with silver pick-up. 'Gloria' – it was a she.

And all the while: music. And as the bunnies and college cold-shouldered, Michael played along to the Foos. He shredded along to Nine Inch Nails, Red Hot Chilis, The Clash, and Lemmy. And late at night, shattered from a shift at the Rubber, he'd hum in his head his own splintering shards of sound. When he played, he was good, and the thin-necked Raptor an easy joy.

But Sheryl, his Mum, was less happy. The guitar sound slashed through the flimsy walls and bled into the house next door. It put the edge on her headache and turned Shania into a cocky, mouthy bitch. Poor Sheryl, she was glad Michael loved something, but she gave him a scarf, a hat and a hot-water bottle and sent him out to the lock-up garages.

Despite the cold and the freezing knuckles, the garage turned into a positive, for the sound drifted out into the road, the wide, treeless main road, and as the boys tricked on their Rip-Sticks, and the racers revved their engines, they listened to Michael's guitar. Kids banged on the door and Michael let them in, sometimes let them have a go. Before long, he had a crowd, and after a few months, when college politely informed him his presence was no longer required, Michael and two others had formed a band and their leader was Muddy Blackmore.

Muddy – like Muddy Waters. Blues cool.
Like Puddle of Mudd. Dirty cool.
Muddy – like Mud and *Tiger Feet*. Retro Cool.
At least, that's what Michael said.

8

DIARY – WELL-OILED WHEELS

Preparation.

Organisation.

Plans.

I was working on publicity – the written kind: posters, press and so on.

Stellar-systematic.

And the word gets out around 'That Place'; "Price is homoing the band!"

Homoing the band?!!

How does staging a gig in a pub translate to sex between men?

This was not the kind of publicity I had in mind; verbal, out of control, exaggerated Chinese whispers.

I stamp on it as soon as I can.

"Sir, Mr Price Sir? How much do you like the band? Do you like them a lot, like *really* a lot? 'Cos that's what everyone's sayin' – homoin'."

"What?! No I don't. Let's be absolutely clear about this. I don't. Only musically. And if I did, it shouldn't be a problem. But I don't, OK? And *'homoing'* is not a proper word."

As the Periodic Table gets glued to books and hands and

foreheads, I ignore the consensus of opinion that I am somehow 'involved' with the band, and focus instead on the boy at the back who's putting his mouth over the gas tap for 20p.

Posters, press and so on.

Got to make this one work.

So I draft some release about their hard-core background, about their thrash/trash pedigree and add "back by surging demand" lies, and include their name. There is a slight debate about this. Nige and Lofty want '*Moist*', whilst Muddy prefers '*Fecund*'. Like a normal person, I'd prefer neither, but as it's Muddy's band, he gets the call. I then take a photo outside the garage. It's sort of OK – taken from below, Muddy close up, Nige and Lofty behind. They look suitably wasted, black-eyed, skinny and spotty. Lofty's holding a plastic water bottle of whiskey, which in the photo, resembles urine. It may well be urine – I never saw him drink it, although he did once offer it round.

They appreciate this sketchy look, along with the press release cock and bull, and suggest they take the promotion "to a whole other level."

"'A whole other level' being what?" I ask doubtfully.

Within half an hour, someone knows someone who knows someone else who has a flatbed truck nearby.

"*You* drive, don't you Mart," states Muddy, snatching the keys from someone's fat uncle.

"Just be careful with her, son," growls Fat Uncle. "She's got a dodgy clutch. Now, here's your fire extinguisher."

"*Fire extinguisher?*" I squeak.

"The engine overheats. And here's your megaphone."

"*Megaphone?*"

"For fuck sake, Mart," barks Muddy and he grabs the megaphone. "*Don't be such a twat!*" he yells into it. "*Get in and friggin' drive!*"

Old ladies by the Bill Hill start in alarm as I crank off round the chicanes with the band swaying in the back shouting obscenities at whomever we pass. Somewhere amidst the obscenities, they manage to chuck in the time and place of the gig, though whether the stray dogs and broken glass take it on board, I'm not sure.

As we head out onto the City Road, quite a few of the obscenities are hurled back, together with 'wanking' and 'dickhead' gestures, and by the time we reach the town centre, a small convoy of teenage truants and Bull Mastiffs are running alongside. At the traffic lights, a few truants manage to scramble aboard and it's not long before I hear the scuffling sound of a fight breaking out behind me.

We bounce along the High Street, the thud of fists and bloody noses against the cabin window. Pedestrians look on aghast as I bump over the crossing, and several times I see the disgusted looks on the faces of mothers I've met at Parents' Evenings. I try to sit low in the seat, keep my head down, but still they stare.

With the engine smoking furiously and shrieking like a wounded beast, the truck grinds back to the estate. I have no memory of how we returned, just a sensation of rigid existence. I creak out of the seat.

Everyone is jumping off the truck and, in a sudden burst of bonhomie, there is much backslapping and laughter. I watch incredulously as the truants disappear with shouts of "See ya there, Muddy!" and "Nice one!"

Muddy, Nige and Lofty are delighted; "Cheers then Mart." "Yeah, cheers Mart. Cool."

Clearly that went well.

They bob off back to the garage where Fat Uncle has been waiting. He saunters over, prises the keys from my stiff, sweating hand, takes one look at the bloodied, smoking truck and mutters; "Fuckin' idiots."

Preparation.

Organisation.

Plans.

It goes on, the more or less conventional process of publicity. Forget about the flatbed. It's posters, press and so on.

Got to make this one work.

So I fly-post. Again. At night this time, in the dark, like a criminal. I *am* a criminal: dodging the headlights, keeping back in the shadows, shifty and shifting from pillar to lamppost.

In the morning, in the light, in the brown industrial sunshine, the posters get defaced, torn in half, covered over with other adverts or showered with the dust from the road.

I go back to the estate, to the Man in the Moon and, like a furtive under-the-counter deal, they agree to "take a load off yer 'ands." Within a day, the posters are stuck all over the boarded windows, over Super-Buy, the Bill Hill, American Nails, a Royal Mail letter box and several parked cars.

That was a *bloody good deal.*

Riding on this crest of opportunity, I visit the Backton Radio Shop down by the dock, armed with an A3 poster and a pile of fliers. It's a radio *shop*, not a station, but still the place to go if you're interested in local news and local music. I can hear the music now as it drifts from all the wirelesses, down the street to the dockside wall. As I step through the open doorway, I see a small knot of people gathered inside around the counter. Rodney – the ex-drummer, and Taser – the other lodger, are eating pasties and dropping flakes of pastry on the carpet, whilst Frankie sits by the till, holding court.

"Well, that just about says it all, eh?" she states in a booming voice.

"Yep, just about," agrees Rodney.

"Orf," Taser splutters.

"Mind me counter," Frankie rebukes, wiping the flakes off with her sleeve.

They turn as I enter.

"Eh, I 'spec you're a bit pissed off about it an' all?" bawls Frankie.

"About what?" I ask.

"This...*this*," she holds up a newspaper and waves it in my face.

It's the Backton Bugle – gossip from the metropolis.

Publicity, press and so on. The well-oiled wheels of organisation: declared, proclaimed, published for all to see; the exact and unabridged details of the imminent gig. Excellent. And the photo outside the garage: Muddy close up, Nige and Lofty behind.

Only it's not.

It's a different photo.

Of a group of people totally disconnected to the gig.

Through disbelieving eyes, beside the band's word-for-word press release, I see a photo of five middle-aged women in majorette costumes, together with the caption; "*Blast your ears out with these gnarly grungers!*"

The photo of Muddy and Co. is on the opposite page.

With a leaden feeling in the cavity of my gut, I read the accompanying caption; "*Nimble ladies display their twirling batons!*"

"Good photo though, Mart!" shouts Frankie. "Against the garage! I like it!"

9

SHERYL BLACKMORE

Sheryl Blackmore had a saying:

"If Mama ain't happy, ain't nobody happy."

She had found it last summer on a fridge magnet, in a little shop by the sea, and somehow it had justified the past. For Sheryl had felt guilty moving out, hastily stuffing the children's pyjamas into a broken polythene bag, and being taken in the dusk to a refuge, by a stranger from a helpline number.

The past was ten and a half years ago when Sheryl had cooked the tea, but failed to wash the socks; when Todd had turned psychotic, beaten the crap out of Steve, aged 11, and taken a pot shot in her face. Since then, Sheryl had struggled to vindicate herself and her disassembling of the family, the home and all that went before: because all *that* had not always been so bad. And at least then there had been them both – Todd and Sheryl, husband and wife, father and mother, a partnership. (Sheryl sugared the memories until the bitterness disappeared.)

But now her nerves were split, as was her lip and the bridge of her nose, and the upper part of Steve's left eye-socket.

In the refuge, people were nice and spoke kindly and, although Sheryl had doubted them, they had assured her she was right. They had called the Nurse, and then the children were bathed in bubbles, fed some hot beans and buttered toast, and tucked up in little beds with some hand-knitted teddy bears. Sheryl had cried though, and so had the children.

A while later, when Todd received an injunction prohibiting contact with his family, he stole some railings from a churchyard and barred up the windows of the house. As he nailed extra bolts to the front door and hid Sheryl's antique clock (inherited from her mother), he thought; "Too right you buggerin' lawyer, and I won't give 'em the steam off my piss." Todd had decided that 'no contact' meant 'absolutely nothing', and whilst he drove the lorries for a mate down on the industrial park, when the CSA came knocking, he cleverly dodged every request for money.

Sheryl was the clever one though, managing to spread her meagre income to provide food, clothes and warmth, Christmas and birthday presents, the occasional gin and orange, and a once-a-year long-weekend in a smelly caravan on the coast eight miles away. It was all cheap and basic, shop's own brand shit, but Sheryl was a grafter, creating four jobs over a six-day week:

Monday – Super-Buy checkout.

Tuesday – cleaning for Old Roger.

Wednesday – shopping for Olive.

Thursday, Friday, Saturday – cleaning at the Man in the Moon.

It wasn't a great life, and there was just years more ahead of the same, with nobody for Sheryl – no Mr Right nor Mr Wrong, but the kids were in one piece, and for that much Sheryl was grateful.

Late at night when she lay in bed and shouts from the street echoed in the dark outside, she took herself away to Old Time America. It was open and light and airy, with the sound of a chapel bell, and the scratch of school chalk on grey slate boards. It was the distant place of stories, from Laura Ingalls Wilder and Louisa M. Alcott. Tatty, sun-browned pages and fading print bought as childhood jumble in a Devonshire village years ago. And whilst she ran on the Kansas prairies and the leafy Massachusetts paths, the lights from the main road faded behind the curtain and briefly, Sheryl was happy.

On a Thursday afternoon, when she'd cleaned and readied the pub for the early weekend drinkers, Sheryl would take herself upstairs to the room above the bar. Here it was cramped and musty, with a nasty fluorescent strip-light stretching across one side. In the centre placed together, were three blue-topped tables, from Backton Secondary School judging by the graffiti scored in the chipped Formica. Sheryl sat with her friends, several women from the estate, on a mixed array of chairs taken from other pubs nearby. Together the women would unpack bags of ribbon and pastel paper, coloured beads and some such stuff scrabbled from kitchen drawers. And as they talked and laughed and teased, they crafted decorative, useless things to gather dust on windowsills. And briefly, Sheryl was happy.

So when the dried vomit on the pub floor turned her stomach, there was the decoupage and the tissue ruffles and the strands of filigree. Or when the splatter on the ceramic was hard to scrub away, there was America in the nineteenth century and the expansive Mid-West plains.

Occasionally, she thought of George Clooney. That would be nice wouldn't it – George Clooney in the scruffy precinct, looking through Super-Buy's plate-glass, watching her subtotal, and beckoning her to follow. Or maybe Johnny Depp, in the exhaust fumes from the cars, taking the carrier bags as she struggled across the chicane to poor old Olive's house.

She thought of the women upstairs, in the room at the Man in the Moon, all sticking and weaving and quilling as the fluorescent strip-light flickered.

And then she remembered the magnet:

"If Mama ain't happy, ain't nobody happy".

And she considered, on balance, she almost was, that perhaps things had worked out for the best, that the children were settled with just her, almost happy because she was too.

And at least this 'almost happiness' was better than a punch in the face.

10

Diary – The Man in the Moon

Lights.

P.A.

CD deck.

It's all in the back of the car.

A logically fitted jigsaw, stowed to the roof, and snuggled up in a protective dirty duvet.

Dave the Disco lifts the hatchback on his practically pre-war Datsun Cherry and begins to haul out the contents. The seats are down in the back and the rear axle buckling under the weight of the gear. Dave, who skilfully hoists the equipment into the road, is about 50, scrawny, scruffy and snake-like, with gelled-back black quiffy hair, a plastic leather-look jacket and too-tight, bollock-announcing jeans. His eyes are small and narrow and his mouth a lascivious sneer.

"Lights, P.A., CD deck. It's all in the back of the car." When he speaks, his throat crackles with tar and his breath is pure Silk Cut.

"I'll hand you these," he passes me two freestanding glitter balls. "And you hand me 40 quid, heh, heh." He laughs smokily and then hacks out a large flob of green sputum onto the pavement. "Nice pair love," he mocks, as I take the glitter balls from his yellow palms.

I'm already wondering if it was a mistake to organise a band *and* a disco for the same billing. Initially it seemed an extra attraction to lure the crowds and, therefore, money well spent. On meeting the DJ however, it seems an extra, highly dodgy expense.

He's still sniggering at the cleverness of his cutting-edge comedy as I stand, wondering how to renege on the booking.

"Go on then love, take your balls upstairs," he wheezes. "There's this lot to take in yet, and *I'm* asthmatic." He leans back against the side of the car, folds his arms, and watches, an expression of unpleasant pleasure on his face.

I squeeze past Derrick the landlord whose corpulence fills the door of the Moon, and as I dither my way upstairs, I hear a beery froth of oafishness between them.

Of course – they know one another.

And Dave is relating his glitter ball joke to a rapturous reception.

"He's one of *them*," I hear him rasping throatily.

"Course he is Dave. Tell it a mile off. Fuckin' gay-un. Still, should be a good bar. 'Av a fag, mate."

The room upstairs is cramped and musty with crass knick-knacks of ribbon and beads drooping from a fluorescent strip-light. The ceiling is dredged with damp, a black dusting of spores spreading from an ugly central patch and falling on the graffiti covered tables – which I recognise. School music room tables. I rearrange them at the far end to stack the lights, P.A., and deck, and by the time I've finished, my hands are grazed and bruised and scraped.

Dave and Derrick gasp their way upstairs. Derrick is carrying the CD deck. Dave is carrying a CD. As he enters, he chucks it on the floor, takes one wicked look around the room and snaps; "'Ere! Woff you done?"

"Sorry?"

"Woff you done then? Woz goin' on?"

"What? What do you mean?"

"Woz goin' on? Wot you fuckin' playin' at?"

"I…I don't understand."

"You stupid poof. I don't do it like that. Oh for fuck sake. Come on, Derrick."

And with angry grumbling and puffing, they begin to lift the tables and the gear to the other end of the room. It turns out there's only one plug-point and no extension cable – as Dave spat in my face; "I'm not a fuckin' electrician."

They disappear off to the bar.

When Muddy, Lofty and Nige arrive, the miserable, squalid setting seems to intensify their spirits. Frivolity and elation clash against the mildewed walls as they push one another with their guitars and scream high-pitched solo riffs. With guffaws and roars, the lads thud down one large amp in the centre of the room, run a flex and two-way socket to the overloaded plug, then slot in their leads, and jam. Nige piles up his drum-kit on one of the tables with a teetering chair alongside, and smashes out a cymbal beat. It's a health and safety horror of epic proportions. It also looks and sounds completely ludicrous – they're neither in time nor standing together. But it's too late now to stop and change: the minutes are moving on, and Shania is waiting by the door, hopping excitedly from one platform boot to the other.

"It's gonna be sooooo good," she beams. "It's gonna be 'lectric. What sort of stamp have you got? I can't wait. It's gonna be hot."

What sort of *what*?

41

Preparation.

Organisation.

Plans. The best laid plans of stupid secondary teachers playing at music promoters.

So I'm standing across the road in Super-Buy, frantically scanning their piss-poor selection of stationery: padded love-heart cards, a deflating foil balloon, string and a *Playboy* calendar. All I want is a hand-stamp, as evidence of payment. And the only available one is on the front of a kiddies' comic. I'll take it.

And then I see something, through the plate-glass shop-front.

Back over the road and down a bit, the mini-cab is stopping. I can see it pulling over, parking up and waiting. And bolt-holed in the back? Bloody hell, it's Aran – Aran, my ex-landlord. What's he doing *here*? Is he doing anything? He's just sitting in the back, not getting out (thank God). I think he's watching, *again*, watching The Moon and listening.

And then I hear something, like the breaking of the sound barrier.

Back over the road, the music is suddenly loud. I can feel it throbbing through the street and I think Aran can feel it too; he's shifting in the back of the cab. The bass is everywhere now, it's throbbing through the tarmac and the drain covers, through the sewers to the checkout in the shop, and as I part with £3.99 (for a copy of *Poppy-Pig Playtime*), I feel the heavy thump of Sabbath coupled with a premature sense of fear:

The disco has started.

I'd been thinking more Justin Bieber, not Ozzy Osbourne,

but it's too late now, the minutes are moving on and a small group of bikers has blocked the entrance to the Moon. Ignoring Aran in the cab, I reach the bikers at the door and squeak through the pressure of leather to see Dave the Disco at the bar, knocking back a pint of real ale. Who's upstairs then, if he's down here? Answer? No-one. I'm standing on my own. The disco appears to run itself, whilst Dave lines up the empty glasses and eyes up teenage girls – of which there are plenty, with the obligatory straws and alcopops and acreage of flesh.

I only went to Super-Buy.

Turned my back for a panicked five seconds.

Now the disco upstairs is vibrating and the bar downstairs is heaving.

I position a chair on the landing, anticipating the crowd. And I wait, and I wait. Then I wait a bit more. But nobody comes: I'm Martin-no-mates. Nobody comes. Not one solitary soul. Not one single, solitary soul. Why bother? The bar is a bigger, better draw than me, and the disco powerfully distinct.

So I'm in the process of anxiety – clinging on to hope but sliding towards regret, just considering if a live band might not compete with the pull of pints and cloudy cider, when Muddy and Co. reappear.

They are pissed.

Right up.

My sliver of hope disintegrates like a salted slug on a garden step.

I should have known (Foos/Dave Grohl song!).

God I wish *I* were Dave Grohl.

I wish *they* were Dave Grohl.

Wouldn't that be great, in the room above the bar? Foo

Fighters in front of my face, rocking the Moon through the floor to the rotten foundations below.

But it's pissed-up Fecund in front of my face, falling about and shouting as they sweep up their instruments to play. Then, at the first smashing chord of Muddy's guitar, there is a stampede in the stairwell and a crowd crushing in the doorway. Thank God. Though needless to say, Shania is first.

"Mr Price! I'm not payin', Sir. I'm with the band!" she shrieks, and squeezes straight past me into the room. She is shadowed one by one, by her ghostly followers who claim through heavy lip-gloss, they are also friends of the band. This is a recurring pattern for several more of the crowd, many of whom are grade one skinheads, and I'm beginning to panic again when I see Taser's long-haired mullet poking out above the throng.

"For God sake, Taser," I pant, pulling him through the crowd. "Stand with me, mate, look mean."

"Eh?"

"Look mean, mate, try and look mean."

It has a positive effect, Taser's sheer height, set jawline and sleepy stare eliciting the money. Soon the punters are packing in and I'm banging down the hand-stamp over and over, with only a few complaints. One biker takes particular offence:

"What the fuck is that?" he snarls, glaring down at the hand-stamp picture. It *does* look strangely incongruous, his two blue/black swastika tattoos, with a ginger cat-face stamp, together with the word "miaow".

Anyway, he goes in, and soon the queue shuffles up to the last couple of people: Muddy's mum (with a large box of out-of-date crisps which she proceeds to hand out to the audience for 30p a packet), and then, shyly, Bruce Boonsby.

"Bruce!" I'm pleased at his unexpected appearance.

"Hello lad. Think I'll stand at the back." And from then on, he stays, right till the end, till the last screaming howl in the mic and the final reverberating twang of a turned-up, feed-backed bass.

The bit in between though, between the start and the close, is not entirely straightforward.

As the damp walls bulge with the size of the crowd, there is one familiar person who manages to keep jostling in and out of the audience. He's a kid, maybe about 17, in his usual dirty clothes. 'Clothes' is generous: they're more 'rags': scuffed-up, worn-down wellingtons, tattered shorts and a soiled sweater that drape his skinny frame like scrappy remnants on a coat hanger. For some reason, not befitting the general outfit, he wears a sombrero, a huge floppy sombrero. He wears it all the time: all year round, even in the depths of winter when a thin layer of frost coats the brim. And all the time he shouts; strange, half-word shouting, like a broken language. "By, by! Come by!" This is 'Farmer-Boy'. A Backton 'name' – a name that the locals know. A Backton 'face' that the locals know. But his home, if he has one, and his background, remain a mystery – nobody knows. Farmer-Boy is a farmer, or at least he thinks he is. He walks around everywhere, all over the town, every day, with a big stick held out as if herding imaginary animals. Sometimes it's sheep, sometimes it's cattle, often it's pigs. Once I saw him 'herding' through the supermarket, shouting his half-words to an invisible drove of horses. Now he's here in the Moon, upstairs, holding on to the brim of his hat, and pushing in and out of the crowd, which lets him. And each time the music stops and the cheering and clapping subside, all you can hear is the shouting and the half-word, farmyard calls of a make-believe cowman with no cows.

After four or five numbers of clapping (and "Come by"), one of the crowd, I think it's the swastika biker, suddenly decides the current state of amplification is not enough. With a heavy shove, he lumbers through to the band, yanks out several cables from somewhere and disappears behind the disco set-up. As Muddy and Co. belt into the next blistering kind-of-chords, the instant blast of music is so loud, I swear the skin on my face is forced back.

There is a collective lion-roar from the crowd and then the pounding starts – the mashing, battering, pounding – up and down, up and down.

I glance behind myself at Bruce. He is pinned against the wall, a packet of cheese and onion in his hand and a look of astonishment on his face. The floor is moving. I'm sure the floor is moving, with each colossal jump, bending and vibrating. Jesus. I'm scared.

I slide warily to the doorway and watch as the floorboards warp with each communal lurch.

Several more numbers pass in this nightmare of lunging, and after what seems like years, Fecund eventually makes its final screech of feedback.

Thank God.

Thank the sweet Baby Jesus.

Thank the sweet Baby Jesus in Heaven.

It is at this point I notice the smoke, floating in a fog behind the disco. And there's another sound. Listen again. Turns out it's me; I'm groaning. Audibly.

Nige, up on his drums, is disappearing in a cloud of grey,

and I can hear his stupid, gormless shouting; "Wow! Dry ice!"

In the gathering mist, a spectral shape shimmers to the plug-point and Lofty squeals delightedly; "Wooo! Look at this! We blew it out! Smokin'!"

He pulls out the cables and, with the last strains of distortion ringing in their ears, the crowd begins to leave. The swastika biker punches the air, taking a swipe at the decorations trembling from the strip-light. As he passes me at the door, he gives me the devil-horn fingers, which I nervously return, trying not to notice the baby-pink ribbon curls quivering in his beard.

For a while, a few of the crowd remain: a skulk of crew cuts, and their mini-skirt girls who congratulate the band with cigarettes and drunken kisses. Fecund can't quite believe it. "What a gig! What a fuckin' gig, man!" And without anybody asking, in a warm haze of happiness, they pack up all the gear, the CD deck, P.A. and lights, and hump it all downstairs, through the door and into the street, where they dump it in the road behind Dave the Disco's Datsun. Then they go, God knows where, into the dark, stumbling off the pavement, with their friends.

And I haven't even paid them.

Back in the pub, Derrick is cashing up, counting the money in coin towers across the bar. He has a seedy grin on his red-veined face and saliva on his chin, and when he flicks down the very last penny, there is a sense of personal achievement in the air.

"Well then, Dave!" he bawls to Dave the Disco who hasn't moved from the bar all night, "Well then, Dave, I done a bloody good job there."

"Yup," slurs Dave. "Me too, mate. Me too."

I interrupt their self-praising; "Right then, thanks very much, I'll be off." I'm just about to leave, with a bunch of fivers in my fist and the chink of loose change in my pocket, when Derrick shouts abruptly:

"'Ang on a minute!" He squeezes his bulk surprisingly quickly round the bar. "Give that 'ere, that's mine!" he rages, and filches the fivers from my hand.

"What? What are you doing?" I gasp.

"Compensation, boy!"

"Compensation? What for?"

"Toilets!" seethes Derrick.

Dave turns blearily towards me. "They're smashed… smashed up," he drawls.

Derrick trudges across the pub and throws open the door of the 'Gents'. Just visible inside, a sink hangs from the wall and a urinal lies shattered on the floor.

"See? That's *your* fault!" he thunders. "*Your* punters!"

And without giving me space to reply, he takes me by the scruff of the shirt and marches me out the front door, slamming it hard behind.

I stand in the night, wondering what on earth just happened. A second ago I had £200. Now I have nothing and still owe the band. In fact, I've *lost* money, having paid up front for the room and the hire of a does-it-itself disco.

The door opens and Dave staggers down the step.

"He saw you comin', mate," he laughs.

"What?"

"'Appens all the time," he splutters, pushing past me to the car. "Every other week it is. Some tosser kickin' it in." He lifts the boot. "He's always nailin' that sink back up."

"Bloody hell!" I'm annoyed. "Why do *I* have to pay? What about insurance?"

Dave turns and stares at me, wide-eyed in his stupor of ale. "*Insurance?*" he whispers disbelievingly. "He ain't got no *insurance.*" Then he shambles round to the driver's side and begins to laugh again, a helpless, liquored laugh. "'Appens all the time! *All* the time!" Somehow, he falls into the seat, and with a rev and resonant backfire, he swerves dangerously away, leaving the boot of the car still open and the disco gear still in the road.

11

GONE TO THE DOCKS

Down by the river, mid-town, where the water shifts as thick as cement, rots Backton Docks.

When life was richer, the water ran clear and trout slipped their way upstream. Once, from the guilt-edged, embellished bridge, a woman saw a porpoise below, its smooth skin gleaming with river-drops. When life was richer, wild cowslips grew here, on the green banks amid rushes and mallow. Merchant ships, their masts straight and tall, would sail in from the Bristol Channel carrying seed and cotton from exotic climes. They would harbour by the dockside wall; thick, rough rope knotted in the iron rings, anchoring the weight. Cabin boys, slight and fast, with the sea in their hair and their hearts, would leap out onto the blue lias stone and shout or whistle their arrival. On these days, the dock smelt of coffee or cocoa, brown sugar or spice. On other days, it smelt simply of air.

Now the dock has no harbouring ships or worldwide trade. There are gulls with predatory eyes. No fish in the river, just a clutch of beer cans in the silt. And polystyrene cups. And now the banks are hard, with patches of scrubby, dead grass struggling through the cracks in the clay, whilst on the slowly shifting water floats a rainbow slick of oil; now the odour from the dock is of caustic effluence.

Two months ago in a late summer storm, when the evening sunlit sky grew dark with low rolling clouds, the dockside wall collapsed. The rainfall had coursed through the streets in a sudden flooding surge, filling the drains and gutters, and the culverts under the road. It had pooled down at the dock where the concrete on the highway had parted from the pressure beneath, like the earth splitting open in a tremor. The concrete had pushed out towards the wall, sending the lias and mortar crumbling to the river below in a landslide of stone and sewage and rubbish from the road. Most of the street had disappeared and all that remained was a jagged edge of road and the narrow pavement at the side.

Now the Georgian flats and shop-fronts abutting the street gazed into the muddy mire that tipped in a precipice beneath their damp doorsteps, and their pink and white painted walls seemed china-like against the rubble below.

The authorities responded. This was an evacuation situation, they stated, on grounds of health and safety. So residents were hurriedly removed with a request to pack pants and prescription drugs, and were escorted from the scene. Then the rumour started, like the words on a bossy parking notice; *"No return within three months."*

Frankie, who owned the radio shop by the dock, freaked out. This was a complete commercial nightmare, a fucking trading fiasco. Were they mad? How was she expected to operate? In 50 years she'd never seen anything like it, for small businesses were being swallowed up by the whale of economic crisis as it was, without a local directive closing everyone down.

As well as this, she was busy: she had a backroom of '40s Bakelite to sort, and a bloke coming round with some vintage batteries. Literally, the town was crying out for selenium rectifiers and silicon diodes, and frankly, the Government had caused the deluge with their slashing of funds to flood defences, and their shoddy maintenance of sewage pipes in lower income areas.

As Backton Radios slipped slowly into the water, its door remained resolutely open, with one or two sandbags to avert further calamity. And the sheer drop from the 'dock-that-was' did not deter the die-hards who tramped their daily path along the pavement to Frankie's old shop. They would come no matter what. It was not so much the obscure radio ephemera that drew them in (though Frankie made sure all stock was displayed for the widest possible appeal: ammeters, capacitors, vacuum tubes, 1930s novelty microphones, wooden Philcos and Admirals, and the odd Honey-Tone Transistor – all lovingly laid out chronologically on upturned Satsuma crates). No, it was more the sense of 'being there' that enticed, or at least, being somewhere: a place specific to stand and talk. And from behind the glass-cased counter, containing soldering irons and wire cutters, Frankie sat like a Sony CEO in a corporate executive meeting, discussing the running of the radio industry and the quality of beer in the Community Club.

The team gathered at the boardroom table was an unsuited, unbooted gang, usually consisting of Muddy, Taser and Rodney and occasionally Farmer-Boy, if he managed to drive his herd up the front step. Sometimes there were others – drifters who'd hang about with nothing else to do. Always someone.

Six days a week, Frankie would multi-task, running the

repairs, her meetings and the publicity of local radio; for this grey-brown toilet-bowl of a town needed music in the streets, and here it was all at hand. In an astounding move of promotional genius, Frankie got it all set up, playing her own revamped radios in a simultaneous broadcast designed to shift the goods. Scratchy antique sounds from the wirelesses balanced on the crates, each tuned in the same, the music transmission spiralling out through the open door and across the whiffy Backton airwaves – all from the old radio shop sliding into the ooze.

And so today is Monday, and again the shop will open. Today is Monday, but the wall remains collapsed. And the other shops in the fragmented street have had to board their doors and windows against the world, to try their trade elsewhere through thin and thinner times. But Monday at 10am, Frankie's back.

The key in the lock is nothing special – an ordinary Yale.

The money in the float is nothing special – copper and silver, just coins.

The carpet on the floor is nothing special – dirty and rising in places.

Yet soon the boardroom table is surrounded by its various execs, all ready with their glowing contributions to the meeting's focussed agenda; the gig at the Man in the Moon.

12

DIARY – THE STINK OF PATCHOULI

Out of pocket.

Out of patience.

Out of my mind.

I must be crazy on all counts.

Ambition? Who wants it! Might as well forget such a mad concept.

Doing things? Nope. I'm not.

Might as well forget it.

And the kids just make it worse. Sanity? Serenity? I have none. When the wind blows, they get over-excited, like cats running round with their tails up. When the sun is hot, they're surly and fractious, like wasps banging on windowpanes. 'That Place' is a part-time millstone. And I'm stuck in its grinding rage, round and round, wearing me down like grain. Today I have the pleasure of being hit on the ear with a rucksack. The kid is an angry Year Seven; small, skinny and picked-on, and by the time he gets to me, science is the last thing on his daily-to-do list. I would have felt sorry; he is pale and late night dark-eyed, his shirt is ripped and he smells of BO. But he flips at a passing remark, hits another kid square on the nose, and kicks a stool into a glass-fronted cabinet. On intervention, he snatches up his bag and hurls it at the side of my head. Yes, it hurts. Then he runs – out of the room, down the stairs, screaming like his clothes are on fire. I see him from the lab window, running through the car park, out the school gate and down the Western Distributor. His Head of Year wants the paperwork.

So I'm trapped here. This is where I am. No running out the school gate for me, alas. Have to keep a wage, because music won't pay my way. Ambition? Who wants it!

Bruce, who listens closely, says not to worry about the money – the money from The Moon and the money for his rent. He can wait, he says, for that. Then, he laughs quietly at my story of school and sadly shakes his head; "Worse for the kid than you." Perspective I suppose. He tells me The Moon was good; "Quite remarkable," are his words. "Try again," he says. "Somewhere else. Be ready for any rubbish."

So I go back to Backton Radios; some idea of advertising, just a felt-tipped stab at self-publicity on one or two fliers and A4 paper. God, the street is narrowing. I'm sure it's narrowing every day, like a cliff-edged hairpin path. I step cautiously, and then over the sandbags to see inside a knot of people again.

If I thought Taser was tall, I was wrong, for next to Wilma the Witch, he's titchy. Wilma must be over six foot, and with her cowboy hat and heels, she must be nearer seven. She is wearing a purple crushed-velvet cape with a skull-shaped clasp at the neck. And her long hair spills over her shoulders in a fruity, rosehip fizz. She is scary from behind, but smiley from the front, with a large mouth and a larger voice – rounded and plummy, well spoken, but with a husky, reefer baritone. The whole effect is slightly unsettling, like John Wayne in drag, but without his ladylike fragility. She looks like she should be American, but she is British to her stiff upper-lip hair. As a girl, she went to Benenden, dropped out when the pot took over and then, "With just a pocketful of wishes and lucky runes, the spirits guided this filly down here." (Malevolent spirits at a guess.) Wilma is a "potion-brewer par-excellence" (these are *her* words, by the way, not mine) and, should you require it, "a spell-chanter and qualified psyche-healer." (Qualified? How do you *qualify*?) On the side, despite her veganism, she works part-time in a butcher's, and plays bodhran in a bluesy-folksy band.

As I enter, she swoops on me with a billow of her cape. "Lordy, you *are* fabulous Martin," she gushes in her gravelly, plummy husk. "I couldn't make it, I was crushing cloves I'm afraid, for a woman who needs a man. But I *have* heard The Moon was a *riot*."

There's a sparkle in her black kohl-lined eyes, and her hair shivers with each enthusiastic emphasis. "*Gosh*, I wish I'd been there. What an *energy* there must've been." Her voice deepens an octave; "*Damn* that *blasted* man. It's going to take a *barrel* of bloody cloves to get *him*, I can tell you. He's not worth it. I did mention this fact, but she wasn't having any of it. Amazing what a bit of money and a complete disregard to the blindingly obvious can do to a woman in love, still, there it is. But *you* Martin, you *are* worth it. Your aura is a sumptuous blue-pink like a morning summer sky."

"Oh! Is that bad?"

"No, no, that's good, *very* good. You absolutely *secrete* positive vibes, darling. Pouring out of you like mothers' milk."

Oh God.

"Now," she turns matter of fact and her voice drops another couple of octaves. "I'd be grateful if you could listen to *me*."

I wasn't aware there was any other choice.

"I have a proposal to make. You can say "no" if you like, but I'll be *bitterly* disappointed if you do."

OK.

"The band I'm in, you know the one?"

"Err…The Tickling Fiddlers in the Forest?"

She winces slightly; "That's right, although we've stopped the 'Tickling' bit now. Trades description, you see. Someone actually expected us to do that and complained when we didn't. It's just *Fiddlers* in the Forest now, although technically we're not in a forest either, but they didn't complain about *that*."

"Anyway, anyway," I hasten.

"Anyway, the band I'm in, Fiddlers in the Forest, we need a gig. A bigger gig, not one of our usual 'three old-timers in a country pub' type of gigs, one of *your* gigs Martin: brim full to bursting and all the power of Apollo. Can you do it?"

"Well…er."

"Oh go on, be a sport darling. Look, I have an idea. You can say "no" if you like, but I'll be *bitterly* disappointed if you do. Why don't you come round to the house, then you can hear us play. We'd *love* that. You've never *really* heard us have you, in all our toe-tapping, hobgoblin glory?"

No, I'd managed to avoid that one.

She flashes me an alluring smile; "We're *spellbinding* darling, and you know *I* can safely say so." She laughs throatily. "Yes, that's what you simply *must* do. Come now, or later if you like, but *do* come. You know the house?"

Who doesn't? It's a squatted, Victorian wreck on the end of a respectable row of well-kept, middle class villas. It's unmissable.

"Excellent. See you about four o'clock then. You never know, I might brew some nettle tea. Cheerio Mart." And with another sweep of the cape, she leaves.

"Gone in a puff of smoke!" shouts Frankie. Her voice is loud and harsh after Wilma's deep, smoky tones. "God, what a stink of patchouli!"

The stink of patchouli is still in my clothes by the time my feet drag to Wilma's. Once again, I'm wondering how this happened; earlier, I was stood in a shop, then by hook and by crook coerced by some spiritualist-medium witch. Was there a yes/no box to tick? I don't believe there was. My pace slackens with each reluctant step and I find pointless distractions to slow me more: a stunted shrub poisoned by traffic exhaust, a cracked shop-window reflecting the scudding clouds. Eventually, with some indefinite resistance, I realise I've arrived at the house. It's in a verdant, tree-lined avenue on the right side of town, no chicanes or zebra crossing, no American Nails or Bill Hill, just a smooth, street-cleaned road and driveway after driveway of neat, tessellated paving and topiary Bay. On every gatepost there's a sign; "*CCTV. Private. Keep Out.*" And in several drives, sleek saloons with city parking permits: easy access to motorway routes, so back for a fleeting weekend bringing champagne and deli-foods. Like cuckoos in blackbirds' nests, roosting awhile then flying off, neither giving to the blackbird, nor conscious of the theft.

And then there's Wilma's place.

It's a rookery.

Broken chair legs and pallets strew the path and drive. There's the rusty camper van with no tax disc, and nearby, the weathered rabbit hutch. The hedges are dark and dense, narrowing the gateway to a slit, and nailed up on the old front door is a dirty, hand-painted notice; "I.R.K. – Independent Republic of the Kindred."

Oh no.

I'm considering a hasty retreat, when the door opens and a man trips out. He is bearded, bare-footed and in pants, and carrying an enormous axe. Waving it uncontrollably in the air, and with a piercing shriek, he brings it down hard on a piece of pallet. It splinters into several shards which shoot at all angles around the drive. He gathers them up, together with a couple of chair legs then disappears back inside, leaving the door open behind. In a second, I hear Wilma's voice; "No, no, Leviathan. Not *there*. Put it on the *fire*, darling." And then I see her in the hallway beyond, looming ghost-like and large in the candlelight, like a clinically obese Nosferatu. I'm shuddering when she bellows my name:

"Martin! *Dahhling*! *There* you are! Don't stand there skulking in the gloom. Come along in, why don't you. That's right."

It's not through my own volition I reach the door: some powerful force moves my feet and pulls my face into a rictus grin.

Wilma nannies me inside; "Come along. There. That's better. Are you cold, dear heart? We've lit the fire. Especially for you."

The hall widens into a big room in which the dividing wall has been partially knocked through, the raw brickwork oddly jutting. And there, in the middle of the clay-tiled floor, surrounded by a few grey breezeblocks, is a roaring, smoking fire. I can't quite believe my watering eyes. It's not in a fireplace and there's no chimney. It's just *there*, in the middle of the room, in the middle of the floor, smoking and choking with fumes. I flap the smoke from my face and splutter noisily.

"Steady on Martin," says Wilma, slapping me heartily on the back. "This is Martin, everyone," she announces, to the vaporous wraiths gathered round the flames. "Martin, meet Titania, Herodotus, Braithwaite, Leviathan and Maureen. Here we all are then."

The fire crackles in the silence and a piece of burning pallet spits out onto the tip of my shoe. Someone moans, "Err…Hello Martin." Then through the smoking fog, I glimpse the open fireplace on the other side of the room – a proper open fireplace with its wide chimneybreast stretching across the far wall. A picture frame without any picture hangs against the ruptured plaster. I point vaguely in the fireplace direction and gasp, "Why don't you use *that*?"

There's an awkward pause for a moment, then someone else moans, "Err…It's blocked."

"…Maybe you could *un*block it," I wheeze.

There's another deathly pause, then Wilma snaps crossly, "I don't think so."

"…Why not?"

"Spirits!"

"…In the *chimney*?"

"Yes!"

"…OK."

A silence ensues, punctuated only by my gulps for air. Then Wilma, with neither signal nor invitation, suddenly begins to sing. Low and deep and slow at first; rich, rough tones; hypnotic chants of persuasion to which the others gradually join. Whilst the pitch and tempo build, and as if galvanised by the urging words, the wraiths move spectrally to the darkening corners, raise up instruments and begin to play.

It is a reverberating sight and sound, eerie in the flame-light and smoking coils. The musicians are standing close together in a revenant huddle, simultaneously vulnerable and bewitching; the beating pulse of the bodhran with twisting threads of violin and breathy harmonies.

When the song quietens to its end, they remain, peering meekly through the mist towards me as if waiting for approval. I thank them, and Wilma solemnly leads me out.

"Goodbye Martin," she breathes in my ear, and closes the door behind me.

I stay on the step awhile and inhale the late afternoon air: grassy, woody and rotting. Then, in the quickening half-light, I hear a soft, flute-like note. As I reach the gateway slit, I look up to the chimneystack and there, perched on the pot, is a pigeon, its little head bobbing as its ghostly, piping voice echoes down to the fireplace below.

13

ARAN

Aran knew a good thing when he saw it. And he saw it that night at The Moon. He had not actually witnessed the band, nor queued upon the stairs. He had not ventured through the door, nor even lingered on the pavement outside. But Aran had seen and heard all that he had needed to.

The sight of the bikers, the crew-cuts, and the girls in short skirts was, at the same time, both repulsing and compelling; like looking at thick-limbed, spiky cacti with artificial flowers. For the men seemed threatening and large, and the women wanton, brash tarts. Aran could not avert his gaze. Bolt holed in the back of a mini-cab, he had watched the gangs as they gathered outside the pub. But as they'd downed their pints and alcofizz amid foul-mouthed disruption and sexual flirting, he'd not had the slightest intention of joining them: along with a primeval feeling of fear, Aran had a subconscious image of a mob of medieval black devils falling on an angel and tearing it asunder. So he watched from the mini-cab window at a safe, unseen distance down the road, somewhere between a dumped fridge and a sprawl of tattered pornography.

In the car, the sound of the music reached him. It thumped out underground to the wheels, the deep thud of a repetitive beat and slashing chords of electric guitar, throbbing through the dark and in time with his blood as it charged from his head to his gut.

Whenever the cheering came, he knew.

Whenever the stamping came, he knew.

And when at last the crowd spilled back outside the pub, he was absolutely certain.

He was going to take his share:

A nice big piece of the pie: a nice big slice of the Communion bread.

Why not?

It wasn't theft, but competition.

Aran, for once, justified himself, although it was no longer in his nature to do so: knocked out years ago.

It wasn't theft, but competition.

Not stealing to take what you're rightfully owed, to take from anywhere, anyone, if you've never had anything else.

Not stealing.

Of all the times he'd needed a justification but never felt the inclination to look, this was the only time he needn't have bothered – business is business, money is money, so why not?

Aran shut his eyes as the mini-cab pulled away and passed the crowd by The Moon.

Not too close.

Sit back.

Sit well back: away from the danger.

Don't look at the thugs, or the skirts, or the morbidly obese.

Aran's skinny toes, prehensile, monkey-like, curled in his tightly laced shoes. His pale, bony knuckles pressed sharply down the crease of his trousers.

Then, out of jeopardy, out on the City Road, he opened his eyes again and watched his exterior world, glasses glinting the reflection of the yellow streetlamps, and headlights of oncoming cars.

It was the regular route; his usual night-time journey along side-streets and non-commissioned roads; through dug-up concrete expanses with the diggers shadowed in the dark; through soulless business parks on the edge of town; past the collapsing dockside wall and piles of rubbish – a horrible reality-tour of ennui and decline.

By the park with the two swings and the old bandstand, Aran peered through the mini-cab window, straining to see a face in the moonlight. And then it was gone as he travelled onto the junction; the bright, fresh glow of white skin, just a sudden recollection.

Through the traffic lights and a hundred yards on the road Eastbound out of town, the mini-cab slowed to a halt.

"Here?" asked the voice in front.

Aran looked out to the building – a down-at-heel, pebbledash place, its triple glazing blazing with fluorescent light inside.

"Yes," he answered softly. "Here."

A full hour he sat, just sat and watched the bail hostel, the double-fronted fortress. The meter ticked the pounds away, but looking *in* the hostel now, instead of *out*, it was well worth every penny. To observe the figures inside as they passed from room to room, was satisfying. Aran thought some were familiar, recognised their bulk and way of walk, or the shape of a skull or width of a neck. To study the crates on the steps, and the empty milk bottles, was a bitter joy. Aran remembered the bread-crate, filled with sliced white each day – his rehabilitative task to spread sandwiches for tea. To stare at the heavy front door with its illuminated keypad and deadlock, was fine. No leaving until 7am, then tagged in the morning sunshine. And when finally the shouts came, as expected, in an aggressive tirade from an upstairs room somewhere, they fell daintily on an easy ear. Aran was smiling, in a way – pleasure, derision and conceit: he was looking *in*, instead of *out*.

Well worth every penny.

They were unfortunate, those inside, he thought – the collared cons and felons. And stupid, as he once was: stupid for not playing properly, that game where only one person knows the rules and wins first prize every time; stupid for losing, forgetting the rules, revealing the tracks and being caught.

Next time, and there *would* be a next time, he'd play the game again, and that time he wouldn't lose, or be stupid, he wouldn't get caught.

Aran had seen and heard all that he had needed to.

And as the mini-cab drove him away from the pebbledash barricade, he knew.

When it passed through the greasy side streets and by rubbled building sites, he knew.

And when at last it took him home, he was absolutely certain.

He was going to take his share:

A nice big piece of the pie:

This time: from The Moon.

And next time: from the park.

14

Diary – Psychos in the Forest

Rowan, fir and hazel;

In bundles;

Tied with twine.

It's all in the back of the van; like a twisted green and brown hedgerow, scythed and gathered and stored for winter warmth.

Wilma the Witch glides to the back of the old camper van and pulls open the rear doors. There is a grating sound of metal, and the large painted letters I.R.K. meet me full on as one of the doors drops back and swings creakily on one hinge.

"Come along then my darlings," sings Wilma. "Out you pop!"

I'm wondering to whom she's speaking (the tree stuff?), when there is a scrabbling from somewhere amongst the greenery and, indeed, *out pops* Leviathan and the others, like a litter of woodland creatures emerging from the undergrowth. They stand in the car park, twigs and leaves in their hair, and goggle at me in surprise. There's a pause as I goggle back. Then something seems to dawn on Herodotus (or it might be Braithwaite):

"Oh. Right. Yeah. Like, we must be here." He turns to the others, his eyes shining through his thicket of hair. "Like, we must be here, yeah?" He meanders up to the arts centre and, as he passes me, says perkily:

"Hi Mart. Cool. Coolio. Cool."

"Yeah. Hi," I manage. "…Coolio."

Coolio?

It is now *my* task, as instructed by Wilma, to unload the van and to "carry the contents forthwith to our ceremonial shrine of artistic endeavour."

"Do you mean the theatre?"

"Yes Martin, I do. Run along quickly now."

Whilst the rest of The Fiddlers condense like an unearthly fog around the bar, I have, once again, evolved from promoter to substandard roadie: I am to haul armfuls of leafage through the front door; through the snug and the cosied-up drinkers; through the spot-lit exhibition room with its displays of "local decorative slipware" (accompanying brochure); through the melee of French café tables and cups of chocolat-chaud; past a baby on a potty; to the theatre. The foliage is spiky and scratches my face, and pine needles barb their way up my sleeves. I leave a trail of shredded vegetation in my wake – on the carpets, in beer, in the potty, and quite possibly in the mouth of someone idly perusing a pile of well-fired clay.

Wilma though, is ecstatic.

"What *fabulous* frondescence," she husks as I drop the last of the hazel at her boots. "I shall transform this dull and dreary space into a fairy paradise." Then she bellows; "*MARTIN?*"

"Yes."

"The theatre shall be my canvas, and the greenery shall be my palette."

Oh God.

"OK," I say.

At the moment, the space looks less like a theatre and more like a potential bonfire. But Wilma happily and obliviously begins to weave the branches around the proscenium arch and along the upstage wall. When she's finished, she stands back and sighs:

"Like a forest-fairy enclave."

There's a silence as she savours her artistry, and then I say:

"...Wilma? Where are your instruments – the violins and stuff? Only, I didn't see them in the..."

With a scream of realisation she's gone, the van keys in her hand and a long stick of fir hooked to the hem of her cape.

Oh no. Not now.

Please, not now.

It's 7.30; it's nearly time.

This stress. I thought there'd be no stress here – in the Backton Orangery: this lovely little gothic place with its gargoyle flower-tubs at the front door, and its smell of biscuits, hot drinks and relaxation.

I'm wondering if it was a mistake, another 'Martin messup', to hire a wasted folk band whose members don't know whether it's day, or if they take honey in their nettle tea. Maybe I should stop this now, put up "CANCELLED DUE TO MARTIN-INABILITY" or "POSTPONED DUE TO FAT HIPPY FUCK-UP".

Should I call Wilma "Fat" or a "Hippy"? Perhaps not to her Mama Cass face.

Oh God.

It's nearly time.

Make a bloody decision.

How many punters for 50 quid?

How many for 85?

Is breaking-even even an option?

I'm still fretting the possible outcome, when Wilma finally returns.

Too late now;

Decision made.

She's back with the bodhran.

And a bloke: who's *that*? Someone I've never seen before. He's carrying the violins, and he's dark and swarthy and dressed in…wait…*breeches*! Like some Bronte anti-hero!

"Martin," heaves Wilma. "This is Heathcliff. Isn't he *gorgeous*? He's mixing the sound."

Heathcliff?

Sound?

Honestly!

Whilst Wilma's bosom lifts in an unnecessary flirtatious display, Heathcliff lopes up to the projection box to do a knob-twiddling act with the sound desk. Only one thing has escaped his notice: there are no microphones or amps onstage and, therefore, no sound to mix. This though, has no bearing on the situation and he continues to create and fine-tune the perfect stereo levels.

8 o'clock.

Time please, gentlemen, time.

The theatre door is open.

And there is a queue of sorts, straggling back through the

slipware like a lop-sided picket fence. An untidy, mismatched line of real ale drinkers and women in fairy wings. Plus a few crew cuts from The Man in the Moon, a flow of long linen skirts, a clutch of short nylon skirts, Bruce Boonsby, Taser and Frankie, and some pensioners who've wandered in by mistake. Wilma follows in last, wafting The Fiddlers along with her arms.

"Come along then my darlings. In you pop."

She herds them up through the proscenium, and so the gig begins.

I'm not sure at which point the stage floor is actually demolished. There are so many points of nadir along the way, they all writhe together like some ugly, demonic dream. At some point at least, I decide to take a breath of fresh air, feeling slightly ill from the smell of patchouli combined with real ale, not to mention the heavy hint of ganja emanating from the projection box and the smoke from the carmine joss sticks in Wilma's fairy glade (not a euphemism). So I'm sitting in the Orangery garden, and thinking how unusual it is to have such an elegant venue in such an inelegant town. And I'm breathing in the lavender and lovage that burgeon by the cobble-paved path, and listening to the miniature fountain and the weighty swish of the wisteria, and it's all very nice etcetera, when I see some people leaving. Only one or two; it's negligible at first. A few have had enough, but then it's more. They file with regularity past the open garden door and, I guess, past the gargoyle tubs to the darkness of the car park. I wonder if it's the pensioners perhaps expecting Bach or bingo or something. Maybe a dope-eyed, spaced-out folk band isn't quite what they'd had in mind for a Thursday evening in a provincial theatre. But when I go back in, the pensioners are pretty much the only audience left apart from Bruce and a couple of 'fairy-wings'. In fact, they all appear transfixed by the onstage show. The show is, admittedly, compelling, not because it's melodic or visually moving, but because it's frankly so utterly disturbing. Wilma is downstage in a spotlight, her eyes shining and her arms rising heavenward as if rejoicing the messianic resurrection. She is wailing deeply in an exaggerated, operatic tone (to be honest, "bullock" and "ditch" are the words that spring to mind, but anyway). Titania is also wailing (though in a high-pitched tremolo style), and playing a violin. Of course, Maureen also wails, but she twangs on a lyre to compensate, whilst Herodotus (or it might be Braithwaite) plucks on a viola with his teeth. This may well be a Hendrix-homage, but he keeps nutting his head on the front of the viola and laughing like a serial killer. As for Braithwaite (or it might be Herodotus), he is beating himself on the chest with two branches from the fairy glade, and roaring gorilla-style, which really is what *I* feel like doing right now, only I'm standing next to an old lady with a Zimmer frame, so I think better of it. *And*, as if all this wasn't enough physical and vocal transgression, Leviathan is suddenly half-naked, save for some soiled underpants, and prancing around the stage playing a flute, and dancing like a distressing cross between the god Pan and Bez from the Happy Mondays.

Jesus, my business career is finished. Already.

What, in the name of all that's holy, have I allowed onstage? No-one, but no-one, will ever buy a ticket from me again, not after this...this...

"Abomination!" announces a frail little voice in the crowd.

Hooray! The old lady with the Zimmer frame is heckling. What else could possibly go wrong? Well...

When this particular 'song' shudders to its desperately anticipated death, most of the elderly shuffle out. The old lady with the Zimmer frame totters softly past me and as she leaves, breathes "Silly bastards," in my face.

Now the auditorium is brim full with no fewer than four people: Bruce, the two 'fairy-wings' and me. But such is the focus of The Fiddlers, they are completely unaware of their lack of audience, pressing on regardless to the next embarrassment, as am I.

It arrives in the reptilian shape of Dave the Disco. Dave, who I suspect is not here for the joy of music, slithers through the theatre door (without paying), and shouts across the room for all to hear:

"Bloody 'ell, look at it in 'ere! It's the fuckin' Fiddlers in the Forest all right! Bloody 'ell, look at all that shit up there; it's not a fuckin' arts centre, it's a fuckin *arboretum*!"

He slides over and shouts in my ear:

"Everyone's round the corner! Cheers for that!" His breath is a concoction of stale smoke, beer and kebab, and he has an oily stain on the pouting crotch of his jeans – I hope it's mayonnaise. He jabs a long dirty fingernail in my chest and continues to shout:

"*Your* lot! All round the corner they are, havin' a great time!"

"*My* lot?"

"Your mates! No, wait a minute, what am I talkin' about? Not your *mates*, your bum-chummin' *audience*!"

"Bum-chumming?"

"All them hairy geezers and weirdoes and skin-heads and shit! Plus some birds; *nice* birds!"

"What do you mean '*round the corner*'? I don't understand."

Dave stares narrow-eyed at me as if doubting my complete stupidity. Then, adopting a baby-voice, lisps:

"'*I don't underthtand*'…Look you stupid idiot, they're round at the Bubble havin' a good ol' knees-up to my disco (fuckin' excellent, by the way), and watchin' that band."

"What band?"

At this point, there's a shriek from onstage and, like a terrifying, murderous madman, Leviathan brings down an axe violently on the stage floor. There is an audible intake of breath from Bruce and the 'fairy-wings' who immediately take ten steps backwards. And, with a splintering crack, the axe cuts through the timber floor. The wood flies out like shrapnel, pointed and jagged and hard.

"*For fuck sake!*" yells Dave. "*He's got a fuckin' axe!*"

I don't know what to do. I'm starting to panic. I'm imagining a crazed scene of blood and severed limbs, and death and destruction and God knows what, when I realise the axe is stuck in the floor. It's stuck fast, the handle sticking up in the air, the blade lodged in the wood. Leviathan can't pull it out and he's tugging frenetically and screaming.

"*He's fuckin' psychotic!*" shouts Dave. "*What d'you give him an axe for?*" He jabs at me again, incensed at my obvious incompetence. "*Fuckin' moron!*"

"Me?" I bleat. "I didn't give him an axe. I didn't even know he *had* one."

"I'm not standin' 'ere talkin' to you no more. Fuckin' Fiddlers in the Forest. Fuckin' *Psychos* in the Forest more like!" And Dave legs it out the door.

Without missing a beat, the 'Psychos' continue: singing and

plucking and prancing. And Leviathan, giving up on the axe, takes up the flute and resumes the tune – unbelievably, the sweetest euphony you ever did hear; light and lilting like birdsong, a dip and rise of blithe, sunny notes. It is a discomfiting conclusion to the show and when at last they ululate the end, Bruce and I are the only ones left.

Wilma swipes the money and The Psychos disappear, despite my protestations at the vandalised floor. I am left to explain the axe to an unimpressed Orangery volunteer who takes the remaining money as liability for damages. Once again, I'm out of pocket. As Dave said: "Fuckin' moron."

Bruce helps me dismantle the tree stuff.

"Thanks Bruce."

"That's all right."

We drag it down to the dock and drop it over the broken wall to wash with the silt and debris, from the river to the sea. Taser and Frankie are there, discussing the 'Fiddler Fiasco' as they stare at the crumbling lias.

"It got a bit much really!" booms Frankie. "All that spiritual shite! We had to go. Sorry about that, Mart." They pick up sticks of hazel and hurl them high in the air, watching them land and ripple the thick, mudded waves. We stand awhile and talk, until the pubs chuck out the last of the drinkers and slam their doors against the night.

It turns out it was Aran:

In a cunning move to make a quid:

At the Bubble Club round the corner:

The very same date as me:

Clever.

Booked Muddy and Co. to play, and apparently raked it in.

"Of course, the Bubble couldn't thank him enough," tuts Frankie.

"Still," lulls Taser. "He was a bit fidgety and blinking. He got behind a table and totally wouldn't come out."

It's then I remember Heathcliff, back in the projection box, ganja-ed to his Bronte breeches and, as far as I know, locked in for the rest of the night!

15

THE BOY ON THE FACTORY FLOOR

When Bruce Boonsby cycles through the gates of the Rubber Factory, he feels a sense of relief: for there is an implicit structure, a kind of order in the sight of the workers as they enter for the daily shift. It is a kind of order which Bruce finds settling, an indication of the day's beginning and subsequent progress. And the steady stream of people, flowing in as pairs or groups, or sidling up on scooters, tempers Bruce's head from the night before and the chaos of persistent thoughts anticipating Susan's return.

So this is an end for ten hours. For ten hours of mixing and pouring and cutting-up, and operating machinery and knuckling down.

Bruce locks his bike in the rack, leaves his sandwiches and flask in a cupboard, and clocks on with his buff-coloured card. Usually there is some sort of commotion: a lively camaraderie of lewd jokes and light-hearted teasing. It starts on one side of the floor in shouts and jeers, then echoes to the other side; a loud smattering of almost-insults, bad language and high spirits. The women are the worst and make Bruce blush – so embarrassed and awkward, he has to turn away for fear they catch his colour they'll tease him even more. Sometimes he'll reply as good as he gets, to make them laugh, which they do; loud and shrill in delight. Most times he keeps quiet and they leave him be.

This morning, however, there is no teasing and no camaraderie. There is only the sound of the heaters – the large metal fans that blow from above, high up in the apex of the roof. Everyone is still and waiting. It seems one of the machines is stuck; the shrink-wrapping machine that covers the rubber products in a thick layer of tight, clear plastic. Its red lights are flashing and its steel plates smoking with a soldering odour. Everyone is still and waiting.

When Bruce draws near, he sees a lad on the floor; he's an apprentice boy, 17-years-old. He is lying in a pool of blood. His overalls, his head, his hands are ripped, and his hair is burnt in clumps. His boots are twitching as the plastic, seared to the skin of his face, melts to the bare bone below. When the water is poured over him, he can barely breathe his pain.

It was part-bravado, part-rebellion gone dreadfully wrong in a mechanised split second. Later, the women tell Bruce in low voices, that the boy had done it as a dare and as a 'middle finger' to the system. No sooner had he been taken on, than he was laid off: the promise of a future just broken in a few terse words. "And it had meant so much to the lad in this bloody God-forsaken dump of a shit-hole town, to be taken on for a 50-hour week and a poxy minimum wage." The women are cross and sorry, near tears, but refuse to cry.

So, it is the last they see of the boy. He goes to hospital and never returns. Unable as he is to work his last week, his pay is docked, and his P45 sent second-class to his step-dad's home address. It's the 'middle finger' back, plus a metaphorical kick in the balls. Of course, it's no surprise there's no money for the boy, no pay, no compensation. "No such pay-out for self-inflicted martyrdom in an economic crisis," shrills someone in the system, in another office miles away. They could've organised a whip-round, but why bother: it wasn't an accident. No need to bother with a gift, nor a card, nor a simple enquiry after his health. Just open a file on the computer and swiftly delete his name.

The day the boy is hurt marks a permanent change on the factory floor. Like an articulated lorry losing brakes on the descent of a 1-in-4 hill, morale speeds quickly downwards. The rumours gather momentum, moving from mouth to mouth, replacing the light-hearted jokes and the usual obscenities with a sense of an ominous ending. By the time the siren sounds at 6pm to close the shift, the tension erupts in physical outbursts of anger: someone punches a hole in a door; someone else takes a knife to a steel-topped bench; a lit match is set to a rubbish bin. The rumours are becoming the truth. *Everybody* says they're the truth. They kick their anger out past the gates, onto the street, and Bruce knows, like the deleted name, the camaraderie is now gone for good, and the structure in his day soon to follow.

God: that poor kid on the factory floor.

The following evening, Bruce and two of the women take the bus to the hospital in the next town. But by the time they arrive, complications have arisen and the boy has been taken away. There is nobody else there for him, so they wait for a while on some plastic chairs in a corridor, watching nurses bustle back and forth, and the stale coffee dripping from the drinks machine. Then they take the last bus home without a word, and that is that.

Over the next few days at the factory, the talk continues of instability and unforeseeable futures, of late payslips and under-wages. So, for the rest of the week, Bruce enacts a kind of plan. He leaves his sandwiches in the cupboard and cycles back to town during lunch. He has to do this fast – lunch is just 45 minutes and it takes time to park and lock the bike, visit the Job Centre and cycle back. And as he's not the only one, the Centre gets crowded and the headway awkward. They could all do this another day or another time, but there *are* no other days or other times – the Centre is shut at weekends and at the close of shifts, so unless they phone in sick and forfeit a day's wages, they all have to go without lunch. Bruce eats *his* on the way home at 6 o'clock, instead of supper.

The Job Centre is orange and brown. Mostly brown though, in the coarse-haired carpet, to hide the dirt from the soles of the shoes. There is orange in places, mostly small ones: the edging of the assistant's name badge. Her name is Sylvia (written in a darker brown). In some ways, the Job Centre is as Bruce remembers from many years ago: the same functionality and pseudo-hope in the cards on the notice boards; the big glass window and the view to the charity shop opposite; the hushed, almost library-quiet as people peruse a possibility; the smell of bodies and resignation. People still take the cards from the boards and put them in their pockets, collecting them up to discuss in a minute. And it still drives Sylvia wild. There are polite reminders on the boards ("Please do not remove the cards"), as she patiently points out, through gritted teeth and a denture bridge. Bruce remembers Sylvia, but she doesn't remember *him*. Bruce had blended with all the others into the dark-brown fuggish surroundings. He also remembers Cynthia, but as Cynthia was the 'last one in', she was the 'first one out' when redundancies came, and has no job at the Job Centre anymore. Sylvia now directs proceedings single-handedly and, frankly, she likes it that way. There is a fervour in her shorthand as she jots down Bruce's details, and a brisk authority with which she dials the number on the card (yes, Bruce had taken it from the board and Sylvia had snatched it back).

"Are you prepared to work shifts?" she enquires.

"Yes I am," he replies.

"Yes he is," she states, back into the phone.

"Are you prepared to work Mondays?"

"Yes I am," he replies.

"Yes he is," she states. "And Fridays?"

"Yes."

"From 6 till 6?"

"Yes."

Sylvia arranges an interview then and there, and smiles icily as she replaces the phone:

"So, to re-cap: the days would be Mondays 12 till 3, and Fridays 6 till 6. The wage would be £6.20 per hour."

Bruce calculates the figures:

"But…that's only…15 hours per week. That's only…"

"£93. Yes? What's the problem?" she snaps.

"Well…I need to work full-time."

"We don't *have* any full-time positions. I'm very sorry, but that's a fact. Now, I've arranged an interview. I suggest you attend." She looks Bruce critically up and down and adds: "If only for experience."

The condescension is also as Bruce remembers, but *this*? *This* is not how it used to be – when you could pick and choose your fancy; when you could leave a job one day, and the next day start another; all the hours you wanted, plus overtime if need be.

There is a queue of school-leavers behind Bruce, all waiting to hear Sylvia's good news of part-time employment only, and a crumbling future of penury. Bruce unlocks his bike and cycles back to work.

The next lunchtime, he repeats the process, and the next, and the next, just in case his boat comes in – up the stagnant river and past the falling dockside wall. His sandwiches are warm by the end of the day.

In the Community Club, Saturday evening, as he sits on the vinyl-topped bar stool, tipping on the uneven stage, Bruce strums the Mid-West ballads and Soft-Shoe Shuffles on his acoustic guitar. One or two women dance, a patent stiletto jiggle in celebration of their night out, glasses of lager and lime held skilfully aloft. Others sing along with Bruce's soothing tones. There is chatter at the bar, and a Club Committee meeting by the door. This time is the remaining part and parcel of his week. And Bruce loves the Saturday evenings: the smell of the cider on the floor; the stickiness of the carpet underfoot; the cold-air draft through the window sashes. Maybe he loves the cheese and onion rolls in a bowl on the bar, or the quarter pints of Rumpley's, or the blue tattoos; the roughness of it all and lack of affection. Maybe he loves Rosie. Rosie blows him several kisses from her seat across the room. She would kiss him for real if she could, at the drop of a teetering fag-ash, but tonight she is trapped between the extractor fan and her old Mum's wheelchair. Her old Mum blows him several kisses as well, then shouts at him to open her peanuts. Rosie opens them for her instead, then strokes her old Mum's face, pats her old Mum's hair, then pats her own. They look at Bruce and wait.

When he sings, Rosie and her old Mum listen, and Bruce Boonsby forgets himself. He forgets Susan, and Sylvia, the boy on the factory floor, and everything else but this.

16

DIARY – BETWEEN THE PLUMBING AND THE RUBBER

Is this *it*?

The end of the road;

The final destination;

Here;

In this bricked-up, asbestos-clad institution;

In this large impersonal hell that smells of copper-sulphate, gas and masturbation;

God I hope not.

Surely dreams can't culminate in just *this* – this daily suffocation from homework, from hormones and over-emotive outpourings. Can it?

When they slouch into the lab and throw their bags on the bench, there is a definable odour of boys' bedrooms and stale Lynx. It's everywhere, like the heady musk of rutting chimps. *Do* chimps rut? It's everywhere. Shania and the other girls can't stand it and kick up, whipping out cans of perfumed spray and spritzing their immediate vicinity. The room is a potential butane-filled fireball – the end of the road now a paean to Impulse and various bodily odours.

Plus someone's been eating garlic bread.

"For fuck sake, Tray, you stink!" shouts a strop with long bleached highlights. And thus it begins: another double lesson of crowd control and loud complaining.

I expected this lesson to go badly. I expect many of the lessons to go badly, yet it's always a surprise when they actually *do*, as if somewhere there's a slight hope I'll trip a switch of enthusiasm. I am trying all the tricks: the visual aids and diagrams; the funny, edge-of-the-seat experiments; the pair work and peer assessment – vesting their interest etc., when there's a disturbance from the side of the class. It's the usual giggling and muttering, and I'm just about to launch in, when I realise what it's all about: there is a flash of orange from outside in the corridor – I glimpse it at the corner of my vision through the windowpane of the laboratory door. And then I see the face, pockmarked and craggy, staring in at the kids: a wild-eyed gaze, a brown-toothed grin, the spikes of the mad-dyed hair tapping on the glass. The class grates to a stilting halt.

"What the…?" I can't help myself; it nearly pops out.

The face catches sight of me staring back, and then a skinny, dirty paw waves, its fingers thick with metal rings.

Oh my God. This is the kind of interruption occasionally mythologised in staff-room conversations, in which a parent set on revenge for a low grade or unfair detention, turns up on the spot to have a mature discussion, then kicks seven shades of shit out of you in front of the students. Oh my God.

There is a murmuring anticipation from the kids as I open the door and go out. I close it softly behind me to muffle the abuse.

"You Mart?" The sudden direct address catches me off-guard and all I can manage is a stupefied, open-mouthed gawp.

I'm gawping: somehow, from somewhere, I know his face, but face-to-face, placing it somehow eludes me.

"'Ere, Mart," the old punk carries on with a series of rapid questions; "You know the Club, right? The Community Club, yeah? And the factory? Well, they're doing this thing, right? Kind of revolution shit and stuff. Only, it's no good without us is it? Won't make any difference. I told them it would be no good – all that candy floss and balloon-animal crap – but they wouldn't listen, yeah?"

I'm totally confused and wondering how he got past Reception, and if he's about to stab me, and whether he's got a flick-knife up his leather sleeve:

"Look, I don't know who you are," I beg. "I don't know what you want, but I think you'd better leave."

"What??" The old punk is incredulous. "I climbed on two bins and through some iron bars to get in 'ere. I ended up in the girls' bogs, which was really dodgy mate, I can tell you. Like some bloody *Carry-On* film, yeah? Typical innit: dirty old perv in the 'Ladies'. Totally by accident an' all."

At this point, Linda Hart (spiky vice-head) marches up the stairs with two 'heavies' from the Estates Department:

"Do you know this awful man?" Linda's voice whips against my addled senses like a swingeing school cane on a podgy backside. The old punk whimpers faintly.

"Er…no…not really…kind of," I falter.

"Oh, for goodness sake," barks Linda. The two 'heavies' grab the old punk under the arms and escort him from the doorway. As they shift him, he manages to shout back over his shoulder; "I'll catch you later, Mart, yeah?"

I grab at the door and swiftly re-enter the lab.

"Did he punch you, Sir?"

"Yeah, did he head-butt you?"

"Did he knee you in the...?"

"No he did not, thankfully," I gasp to the excited faces all now looking my way and eager for information.

"He were a right old filthy tramp, weren't he, Sir?"

"Was he your boyfriend, Sir?"

When the bell rings for lunch, I'm not sorry. The lesson is difficult to salvage after all that. The kids are just too hyped up on smutty innuendoes and teacher-insults to fully embrace the subject of fractional distillation.

In the canteen, the queue is disordered. There is a bunching-up of bodies and people pushing in. It's peak-time and the room heaves with teenage appetite – a manic crush of salt and cola cravings. Eventually, I manage to obtain an unnecessary extra helping of chicken curry. Beryl likes me for some reason, and piles it on my plate in a weighty, mould-like mound. She then shovels chips on the top and hands me a plastic fork with as much delicacy as if she's handing me a seaside spade.

"Get stuck in, love!" she shrieks. The other dinner ladies whoop in joy and I leave as quickly as I can.

By the time I get to the car, the food is almost cold, and oil separated to the rim of the plate. I sit in the driver's seat for a moment of isolation; just me, and the dish of stroke-propellant balanced on my knees.

So I'm listening to the radio and pushing the pale food about with the plastic fork, mindful of the time and my encroaching lesson of acid titration, when there's a crashing sound of metal, and a nebulous blur in front. Jesus! Through the windscreen right in front of my eyes, a blur of orange smashing down on the bonnet like a block of concrete from a high-rise car park. I jump so much, the plate flips over, smearing the floor with fat. Cold curry is seeping through my socks. And there, grinning through the glass, is the old punk. Grinning and gurning, splaid out on my car as the music from *The Archers* rings out.

"All right, Mart!" he shouts. He slides off the bonnet like wet road-kill then, without asking, opens the passenger door and climbs in.

"Phwoar! What a stink of curry!" He peers at the congealed mess in the foot-well, then leans down and picks up a chip. It is peppered with grit. He holds it before my nose:

"Do you want this? Only, I don't wanna be rude or nothin'." He pops it in his mouth as if it were a Belgian chocolate truffle, and chews meditatively:

"Hmm," he says. "Is it time? Must be by now. Turn off this drama-crap and fuckin' listen to Backton!" He fiddles with the knob on the radio, leaving a film of grease from his filthy fingers. "Where is it? Where's the bloody thing?" He's chuntering to himself and spitting flecks of chip on the gearstick. Suddenly, the music blares out. "Aha, goddit! Listen to this, yeah?"

As a raging, tuneless tirade of chords and growling vocals blasts my puny speakers, the old punk reclines back in the seat with another brown-toothed gurn. Close up, I realise he is wearing 'Stay-pressed' trousers and, under his leather jacket, a white shirt and a 'George at Asda' tie. Using his metal-ringed fingers to help, he lifts his long, skinny legs and rests his feet up on the dashboard. Beneath the 'Stay-pressed', he is wearing ox-blood Dr. Martens. They are '14 holes'. I count them. Each one: because I have lost the capacity for speech. Only a matter of seconds later, there is silence. Then there's the scuffling of a missed cue, and the DJ's voice booming out in mono:

"That were our local chart-toppers, 'Urge the Scourge', loud and proud. Catch 'em on CD, available in town somewhere!"

The old punk sighs, a rotting, un-flossed, stale-food sigh.

'Urge the Scourge', it transpires, is spelt 'Urge the *Scurge'*.

"For lexicographical symmetry," he says primly, sticking his pierced chin in the air with pride. "That were *my* idea. A bloody good one, yeah?" He gives me a sideways look, checking for any dissent, then carries on: "It were *all* my idea, Mart. Urge the Scurge is…" he lowers his voice, "…*my baby*." (A rather aged baby as it happens; a 26-year-old, *ADHD* baby, if the parental genes are anything to go by): he cackles loudly and stomps his feet madly on the dashboard. "Yeah, that's right, *all* Paddy's idea."

(Of course – Paddy the Punk!)

"My brainchild, it were." (His evil, belligerent brainchild conceived back in some God-knows-where, out-of-the-way place.)

"In Bleakhill. Do you know it…? No…? Not surprised. Deepest, darkest, edge of Exmoor settlement." He glances out of the window and sniffs derisively; "Weren't many punks about *there*."

I'm wishing there weren't any punks about *here*, stretched out in my curry-covered car, but Paddy's suddenly mid-flow with his life-story and I'm worried about the silver knuckle-duster on his right forefinger and its proximity with my lower left jaw.

"We caused a lot of consternation at the time," he continues. "Me and my pals. I mean, one minute you're lovely and honey-pie, the next minute it's like you're from Dante's fuckin' 'Inferno'."

The Circles of Hell are nothing compared with this – the punk biography out of the blue. But he keeps going, telling me how they'd morphed, Paddy and his pals, overnight, from school-suited boys with candy cigarettes, into drainpiped, spitting teens with guitars slung on shoulders, like guns.

"People didn't like us. A notice was put on the shop door – "*NO PUNKS HERE*", which was ironic really, 'cos actually there was four of us: me, Jimbo, Lanky and Si."

And when the boys jammed together at the weekend, in Si's bedroom or Paddy's Dad's shed, there were village complaints and gossipy fall-outs till parents banned the band, and the boys turned to religion to fix it all.

"Christian benevolence it were. We would practise in the Church Hall on Thursdays after school. And other times as well: as much as we could really. Funny I s'pose: amongst the crucifixion pictures and teacups. Vicar let us. He didn't mind. Getting youth in, and all that. Good bloke. Dead now though: shot himself."

"Jesus!"

"No. Suicide."

So Urge the Scurge became a household name of sorts, in Bleakhill anyway. And by the time Lanky had learnt to drive, and somehow acquired an old Chevette, the band had decided to take their name to the culture-clamouring masses.

"Which was where?" I ask.

"Tiverton."

Obviously.

Tiverton, of all places, was bound to delight in their honed repertoire of two-minute, three-chord, punk-filled venom.

"To be honest, Mart, we were never Van de Graaff Generator. Anyway, Bleakhill made Tivvy look like L.A., and some people 'got us'. Most didn't. But we kept going. And here we are."

"*Backton*?"

"Where the wind picked us up and blew us, I s'pose. Still: no money in it, so we got jobs. Do you need your windows cleaned?"

"I don't think so."

"Pity, I've got all the gear. Any auditing requirements?"

"*What*?"

Urge the Scurge still jam. It's what they do: punk classics, and their own. They 'rock it out' for pleasure between the windows and the audits, between the plumbing and the Rubber. It's what they do.

Paddy sticks his Doc in the side of the door and pushes it open with his foot. "So, you'll sort it, yeah?" His orange spikes scrape the edge of the car roof as he gets out. "It'll be better with us, won't it? More of a ...*statement*."

He turns and bounces towards the school gates, the '*anarchy*' sign on the back of his jacket attracting comments from the students who follow him. They point and shout, and he shouts back. It's then I realise they're *my* students, from the lesson I should've been teaching half an hour ago. Then I realise something else: there's a huge dent in the bonnet of my car, a huge dent from Paddy's head. Oh well, I suppose it's "more of a ...*statement*".

17

FROM THE VIEWPOINT OF A STARLING

The chimney at the Rubber is going to be brought down. At least, that's the substance of the rumours. Muddy wipes the soot and grime from his eyelids as he looks up at the Victorian monument. Sometimes the pinnacle is invisible in the midst of the factory-fumes that plume with the breeze to the town. The tip of the chimney then peeks for a while as the fumes disperse in the air. It has the sensation of movement, looking up at the tower above. It seems the chimney glides the other way, the other way from the fumes, the opposite way from town. And Muddy likes this odd sensation. He wipes his eyelids again with the back of a dirty sleeve. It's possible he might be crying, but you couldn't say for sure, and anyway, he would never admit to *that*. Not done *that* since Mum switched off Kurt Cobain on 'cable'.

There are starlings flying over the chimney, in a dark black flock against the clouds. If it wasn't for the traffic in the streets, Muddy thinks he might just hear their wings. He wonders what the top of the stack looks like from up in the sky, from the viewpoint of a starling. Maybe the soot-speckles glint in the morning light, around the chipped edges of the chimney pot.

Or maybe, he thinks, it's not so good: the bricks streaked with mould, and mess from the predatory gulls.

The starlings nest by the factory, on the neighbouring scrubby waste-ground. They peck at the rubbish and the debris, finding sweet crystals forming in the skips that are warmed by the factory downpipes. Muddy wonders if the birds will leave when the chimney comes down, and when the site is sold for development. Why stay *here*, if you're a starling, when you could open your wings and fly anywhere? "That's just weird," thinks Muddy. "I know where *I'd* fly: Seattle, baby! And California. Too right! I'd fly over the Golden Gate Bridge and up in the Santa fucking Monica Mountains."

When he returns to work after this brief morning break, a change has taken place in the factory, suddenly, like a hairline crack in a rock-face splitting open to the salted winds. The furnaces have been shut down, and the production lines switched off. Workers stand and wait whilst supervisors take their orders from above. Rapidly, the circumstance is exposed; get packing-up the Rubber, 'cos there's nothing else to do.

So the wheels in the factory wind down, and the workers do a 'go-slow', to extenuate their time and their money, what's left. Muddy finds himself back outside, in the long shadow of the chimney, with a wheelbarrow.

As the last of the plumes die away to the river and the dockside wall, bricks come plummeting down. His job is to pick them up and dump them in the skips. It's a laborious task, backbreaking, and painful without gloves. By the time they reach the ground, the old Victorian bricks are just terracotta fragments, deformed and acicular. They snag at the skin on his fingers, pushing the grime beneath. When he clatters the shattered brick in the barrow, the birds fly out from the scrubland, startled by the sound, and rats dart from tangled brambles and over the toes of his boots. This is a task he'd gladly exchange for that of 'chimney dismantler' – up there, near the sky and the sunrays, with the starlings overhead. And if it was *his* task, he'd chip at the mortar like an archaeologist in a Roman trench; delicately, reverently, and lift the bricks out one by one, then dust them with a soft-bristle brush. He'd lay them in a canvas sheet and winch them safely to the ground, complete and intact. Not hammer at them with a mallet indiscriminately till they relented, fragmented and crashed down.

By lunchtime, the end of his shift, Muddy's hands are hot and cut. He cools them on the factory downpipes, the metal now cold with production decline. Then he picks up a piece of brick, drops it in his pocket and keeps his hand gently around it.

Outside the factory gates, Muddy wonders if he'll ever go through them again. Forcing himself not to look back, he trudges wearily home, at the side of the street as the traffic rumbles by on its way to somewhere else. Any closer, it would pare his knuckles, but he's oblivious to the trucks and the lorries, and the wing mirrors that skim his hair. His overalls crumple at his ankles and scuff the tarmac as he reaches the City Road. His boots are unlaced and loose.

At the precinct, his nose against Super-Buy's window, he sees his Mum in her tabard, at the checkout. She is putting through a packet of Oreos and a jar of instant coffee, plus other stuff he can't quite make out. She sees him and she waves, and he waves back. When he goes in, she lets him take some crisps and leave without paying. Then he stands on the pavement and eats with dirty hands. He likes the MSG, the calcium chloride and saccharine. It's tasty and cloys at his tongue, the flavour harsh and intense, and the crisps clod in his teeth and at the back of his gums so he has to pick in his mouth with his fingers.

By the time he's screwed up the packet and thrown it in the overspill from a bin, Muddy has made up his mind to enact a kind of plan. It's only a *kind of plan*, but he thinks it might have some promise. He scuffs past the Bill Hill with its racing commentary blaring from the open door, past the Man in the Moon with its lunchtime drinkers and the sick in the gutter from last night, and all along the main road till he reaches the Western Distributor. Up here it's a fast road, and another walk – another scenic walk by the local attractions. He scuffs past the school and the peeling-paint gates and the kids shouting a cocky invective, and on past the magistrates' court, till he sees the bunnies, tripping from college back to town. They are bright, glossy-haired and chatting. Muddy has to make way on the pavement for they walk in small groups and there's not enough room for him too. This time, he walks *on* the carriageway, *against* the oncoming traffic, against the cars and the artics for another two miles till he reaches the college entrance. (It's only *a kind of plan*.)

This is the subsidiary college: small and ugly, several portakabins by a cemetery, where the Western Distributor branches to the motorway roundabout.

As he waits in the reception area, he thinks, "It's better than last time. Floor's cleaner, I reckon. And roses in a vase." And he thinks it's lighter somehow, maybe new emulsion or something, which creates a sense of openness in the restricted space: he likes it.

The receptionist finishes her phone call and eyes him with suspicion. He is a tall, filthy smudge against the barley-white walls and buffed floor: she doesn't like it.

"If you've come about the drains, you need to wait outside," she says smartly. "If you don't mind." She has a fashionably large cup of skinny-latte that she covers with her hand as Muddy leans over to talk.

"It's not the drains I've come about. I want to come back. You know, study and stuff; start again."

There is a pause as the receptionist stares and re-evaluates the situation. Then she slaps down a piece of paper on the desk; "Here's a form. Fill it out. Write clearly please."

Muddy borrows a pen. It's not the receptionist's floral-patterned fountain pen. It's a spare pen for the hoi polloi. She watches him critically, judging his writing, inwardly surprised at the speed of his hand.

When he finishes and submits the form, Muddy waits for some further directive.

"Goodbye," says the receptionist precisely.

"Oh!" says Muddy, confused. "Do I not see anyone?"

"*See anyone?*" replies the receptionist. "*Now*? Oh no, that's far too premature."

Whilst rearranging the roses, and with some satisfaction, she apprises him of the full facts: that as an ex-student, he is not a priority; that the deadline for the next intake has gone; that he needs to pass a 'preliminary stage'; that they'll contact him in due course which is unlikely to be for ten months.

There are other lads younger than him carrying lever-arch files thick with notes, and trendy Air-Force bags heavy with textbooks and coursework. They know shit already that Muddy will never know, and he knows *that* much. They take no notice as he walks away.

In the garage, in the afternoon, as the shafts of light point under the doorway, Muddy sits amongst the car-boot jumble, and hears the jagged chords. He replays them to himself, unamplified at first. Just the twanging of an unvoiced guitar, and the squeak of his callouses searching the frets and the strings till he replicates the sound in his head. There is something about the half-light and the quiet, tinny sound that muffles the day outside and the traffic swerving round the chicanes, and the shouting, and the barking, and the noise. Perhaps it's the smell of the old paint and tyres and plastic bags, and the fusty, moth-eaten junk tucked away in corners, that trick his mind. Pavlovian in effect: see this, hear this, smell this, and the rest will fade away. Or, most likely, it's the movement of his fingers as they flit quick and agile, and the feel of the threads of steel, and the wooden neck in the crook of his thumb.

When Nige and Lofty arrive, the sudden sound of their fists banging the aluminium door makes him flinch, and when he pushes it open and the light pours in, he has to close his eyes, for the glare is painful and incandescent.

So, with the door shut back down, they jam good again; for hours. Till there's no day seeping through the cracks, till the friends are no longer even shadows, but just a sensory notion to one another. Then, in the pitch, as the last chord reverberates off the tin buckets and pots of paint, Muddy asks:

"Where would you go?"

The other two stop shifting in the gloom, and pause.

"What?" gruffs Nige.

"If you were a bird," says Muddy. "Where would you go?"

Another pause.

Then Lofty pipes, "If I was a *bird*? …Like…a *girl*?"

"No, dick-head," says Muddy. "I mean a *bird-bird*. I don't know which one. *Any* one. A starling."

18

DIARY – PUNK BIZ

Bald tyres.

Reversing.

Over the grass, the neatly mown grass.

They carve deep muddy tracks in the playing field: long, deep tracks, gouged from the road and across the green.

As the gears grind and the exhaust chokes, the truck forces backwards into position. Once stationary, it sinks a little way in the ground, then the door of the cab squeaks open and, with a good deal of huffing and puffing, a short round ball of a man lumbers down.

Oh God. I don't bloody believe it.

Shit, I know who that is.

It's Someone's Fat Uncle.

Someone's Fat, Laconic Uncle.

With his clapped out flatbed – the one in which I screeched Muddy and Co. round town in a bizarrely violent stab at self-promotion.

Fat Uncle surveys his parking for a moment, then, nodding in satisfaction, slogs over in my direction. His bulbous gut shudders beneath his grey vest, and his nasty shoulder hair fluffs in the breeze.

Oh God, I remember that day; the big punch-up and the smoking engine, the blood on the rear window. Unfortunately, so does Fat Uncle.

"Oh, it's *you*," he remarks grimly. "Bunch of fuckin' idiots."

"Hello there," I say sunnily. "Thank you ever so much for the loan of your truck once again. We'll be very careful with it today."

My niceties are of no consequence, however. Fat Uncle shakes his fat head and mutters something offensive, then disappears to the Cider Tent.

Oh God. Fat Uncle's flatbed.

Urge the Scurge are playing on the back of it later, as part of The Community Club Festival. I managed to 'sort it' for Paddy. Now I'm recalling his head-dent in my car bonnet, and can't imagine 'careful consideration of the truck' will be high on his list of priorities.

As I'm predicting the possible outcomes (insurance claims and litigation, plus the weight of Fat Uncle's cider-stoked gut as he pins me to the ground and pounds his fist on the bridge of my nose), I hear a nasty, sly voice behind me. It's pointed and sharp and deliberately pitched to be heard across the widest vicinity.

"Piss me! Look at all this then!" Dave the Disco's speech Silk-Cuts into my ear; "I mean, pissin' 'ell, it's a step up for *you* innit?" He appears beside me, rippling his tar-stained fingers through the air like a magician performing a trick. "Look at it all, eh?" He ripples round at the stalls of homemade cakes and knitted toys, the kiddies' teacup ride and the Lucky Dip. "You've hit the Big Time now mate, eh? Glastonbury friggin' Festival innit?" With a rough cackle of glee, he claps his hands together then rubs them up and down on the front of his thighs.

God, I really wish he wouldn't stand so close; I can almost *smell* disease. His jeans are dirtier than ever, still with the oily stain on the jutting crotch, plus an additional smear leaching down the inside leg. I feel a manic Tourette-ish compulsion to scream the words "Bollocks!" and "Persil!" but suddenly, he's getting closer, coiling a skinny, invertebrate arm around my neck and then, as if I were a Pre-War housewife choosing a frock, he says; "So, what you puttin' on today then love, eh?"

"Err…" I hesitate, disarmed at his matiness attempt. "Kind of…punk."

"*Punk*?" He looks round disbelievingly. "What is it? 1977? Fuck me, cuttin' edge, eh?" He cackles out at the small crowd of onlookers who've quickly gathered to enjoy my rapid crash of dignity. "Christ, you've hit the Big Time now – doin' the punk biz in Backton. What is it next? U2 and that Bone-oh?"

For the last swathe of shame, he addresses his audience directly whilst also pointing at *me*; "Here he is look, givin' Harvey Goldsmith a run for his money. Friggin' Live Aid, innit? Piss me, he'll be pullin' it in now. Job's a fuckin' good-un!" He ruffles my hair with a smoky hand then slithers to the cider.

As the last of his foul-mouthed curses vibrates the air, I'm left hyperventilating with embarrassment. If only I'd had the inner confidence to take a chocolate cake from the nearby stall and ram it heavily in his face. Or even just the confidence to *warn* him that I might. But his supporters are stocky and mean. One or two of them, keen for more profanity and humiliation, slither with him to the alcohol. I hope I'm mistaken, but I'm sure I heard Fat Uncle laugh. I look over to the Cider Tent and there he is with Dave. Dave's boasting of his own rudeness and my denseness. They're propping one another up whilst simultaneously supporting the brisk trade in cheap pints of cloudy Perry. Fat Uncle is getting stuck in and his vest is riding up.

"Never mind, lad," says Bruce, after I've paced the field to recover. "He's all mouth and no trousers, that man. He's louder than his own disco."

Dave's disco is, incidentally, now blaring out over the entire town – a constant loop of Van Halen, Bon Jovi, and *Agadoo*. One thing's for certain though, he knows how to win a crowd whilst covertly chucking back the booze and fags – people are loving it; they're singing along and dancing, punching the air and waving inflated condoms with "*SAVE OUR RUBBER*" written on in ballpoint. Generally having a good time.

And Bruce is having a good time. He's sitting in a deck chair, despite the easterly wind, with a picnic cloth on the ground, and Rosie pouring tea. With them, wrapped in a blue-checked blanket, is an old lady. She is sat in a wheelchair and blowing kisses to passers-by, then dropping her top dentures for a laugh! I don't know if Bruce realises it, but whenever he laughs with the old lady, Rosie joins in. And Rosie pours his tea into a china cup and stirs it for him with a silver spoon, whilst her own tea is in a mug, and the handle broken off.

I sit with them for a while, on the edge of the picnic cloth, and Rosie hands me a slice of cake:

"It's Battenburg," she says brightly. "Mr. Kipling."

I haven't the heart to refuse.

The next hour or so passes fine. At least, I *think* it's fine.

Boding well.

The future good, maybe.

I allow myself the luxury of believing this, anyway.

Hot dogs and burgers are consumed, kids run riot round the stalls, and the teenagers loll on the grass. Muddy's mum looks on disapprovingly from behind a stand of knick-knacks whilst Shania and her friends roll half-dressed in the damp, flirting and fooling with some boys, and screaming high spirits to the world.

At some point, Dave and Fat Uncle show similar high spirits. In an unsteady blur of drink, and under the licence of "It's *my* fuckin' disco and *his* fuckin' truck", they clamber aboard the flatbed.

"I'm gonna do it, mate," says Dave.

"I know you bloody well are," says Fat Uncle. "Good on you, my son."

"I'm gonna rock this fuckin' place," says Dave.

"Fuckin' *tune!*" shouts Fat Uncle in appreciation as *Livin' on a Prayer* blasts out.

Karaoke is their apparent intention and Dave, spotting the microphone 'downstage', attempts to pull it from its stand. Fat Uncle is still struggling up the side of the truck when Dave finally yanks the microphone out, hitting himself in the teeth as a result. Then, amidst a screech of distortion from the speakers, Fat Uncle, having now scaled the summit of the truck, tries to grapple the microphone from Dave's hands. What on earth? I didn't book a bloody support band, but here they are like a pair of preening pop-tarts vying for TV airtime, both desperate to display their talents. And again, the people love it, gathering around and cheering as the pop-tarts bellow like boars. I can't get over it; Urge the Scurge are about to be upstaged by a couple of cidered old sots with all the musical talent of a turd, and to be honest, that's 'sexing' them up.

In the background, the disco blares. It's getting louder it seems, pumping out like fairground sound. And as the barrels steadily empty in the back of the Cider Tent, so the fairground sound pulsates, the singing and cheering build up, and the quids stack up for the Rubber and the workers like Bruce and Muddy. Muddy is somewhere around, showing solidarity for the cause, still in his factory overalls.

So, I'm desperately hoping the future's good, boding well etcetera and all that, and then I see Aran. *Aran*? It can't be. I do the classic double-take, cake halfway to my mouth. Is Aran really *here*? I'm not expecting him to show his face after his night at the Bubble that time. But he's definitely here all right, just standing over by the teacup ride. I'm willing him to go away, before he takes the crowd to a better gig. That would be *really* great, wouldn't it, a festival left with four onlookers! Thankfully, he sees me seeing him, walks off and then he's gone. Disappears. *Thankfully*. It's almost as if he hadn't been here, and so I let myself forget.

For a while longer, I sit with Bruce as the 'act' on the lorry continues. I think it's just me who finds their karaoke quite frightening; everyone else keeps cheering along.

When Urge the Scurge arrive, Dave and Fat Uncle are still bellowing, and Rosie is still plying me with cake. I am stuffed with Mr. Kipling's additives, and feeling slightly sick.

"All right, Mart!" shouts Paddy, slapping me hard on the back. "Where can I put me Granddad?"

Where can he put his *what*?

I force down the last bit of Battenburg, and turn round to see Urge the Scurge (leather, bondage, and a bottle of Gaviscon), and standing between them, a little old man wearing slippers. He is wobbly and frail and they are holding his hands and gently stroking his arms.

"Can you get him a chair?" asks Paddy. "Can he sit down, at the front, near the speakers?"

Near the *speakers*? What? Are they mad?

"Near the *speakers*?" I say. "Are you mad?"

"He likes the music," replies Paddy. "Don't you Granddad?"

"What's that?" creaks Granddad.

"The music. You like it."

"Oh-ahh, I do."

So whilst the last of the disco blasts out and Dave and Fat Uncle stumble off for more Perry, Granddad perches on a folding chair by the side of the flatbed truck, bang in front of a shonky speaker. His face is a picture of light as *Livin' On a Prayer* soars out for the millionth time across the field. And when the band finally takes to the stage, hammer-clawing out their first chords in a serrated, tuneless mess, Granddad doesn't turn a hair. A number of people move away, further across the grass to the teacup ride and toys, but Granddad can't get enough. As the sound knife-stabs out of the speakers, he's nodding his head and grinning, tapping his slippered feet as the drums veer ferociously on and off a beat. After a while, he's joined by a couple of kids and a small local posse of 'hoods' who proceed to pogo and mosh to the band's cover of *Too Drunk to Fuck*. Grandad smiles along serenely.

I don't know whether it's Urge the Scurge, or the sight of a pensioner mouthing the words to Bad Brains' *Pay to Cum* that attracts the police, but when the blue lights start flashing along the road, I begin to wish I hadn't eaten that last bit of Battenburg cake.

It's almost a trigger when the cars park up and the police run across the grass to the site: a wordless provocation. From the Cider Tent and old deckchairs, a swell of people moves to the flatbed truck and begins to shout – a boundless barrage of comic obscenities and abuse, personal and pornographic. But not at the policemen – at Urge the Scurge. And throwing stuff. Any stuff: plastic pints of cider, coke cans, clods of earth, and even an orthopaedic shoe. Where it comes from, I have no idea, but it flies like a grenade and catches Paddy on the chin. Not that he minds. In fact, he's laughing. A lot. And when he lobs the shoe back out, hard and high across the heads of the crowd, the audience begins to chant; "*Scurge! Scurge! Scurge!*" It is an intimidating vocal noise – loud and strong and nearly aggressive, but it only encourages the band. They launch into another punk medley, racing through the chords like whipped horses in a steeplechase.

And then the police wade in.

It is more a Cine-camera collection of moments, the ensuing events – "Memories from my Life," by Dazed Promoter, available on clueless.com, no doubt to be posted up from the various mobile phones immediately being held in the air.

Mid-crowd, there is some kind of scuffle – a pushing and falling over. Then the orthopaedic shoe reappears. I glimpse it tossed on the wave of people, like a bottle on the sea, then down by the truck, beating against the door portside, denting and thudding at the rusted steel.

I'm looking round for Fat Uncle, fearing his cannonball fist, but all I see is Paddy, close up, suddenly, like realisation. He's off the stage now, handcuffed, frogmarched, and bent over the front of a police car and yes, there it is – the Paddy trademark. Oh God. His head. He's banging it down on the bonnet, over and over again – the crunching sound of a skull on a brand new Ford Focus TDi; belonging to the police. Oh God.

Despite this, Urge the Scurge are still chain-sawing their way through an (im)pertinent covers collection – *Anarchy in the UK*; *I Fought the Law* etc., and in the middle of the chaos, benign and mild, remains Paddy's Granddad, sitting sweetly at the front, beatific, gracious, enjoying the afternoon as if it were an elderly people's tea dance.

When Farmer-Boy appears, chugging along the road, arms out guiding an invisible herd, I'm considering an elderly people's tea dance an attractive possibility for my next promotion. The policeman is just about managing to bundle a livid Paddy into the back of the vehicle as Farmer-Boy draws up beside him. Then I hear Farmer-Boy say; "'Ere, Officer, I got me cows round the corner. They're movin' this way and I won't get 'em past that car. Can 'ee move it over please?"

After a bit more Paddy-bundling, the policeman gets in the car and moves it over to the side of the road whilst Farmer-Boy vanishes back the way he came. A minute later and the policeman is standing at the roadside, waiting for the cows to pass. Then, from around the corner, the sombrero yanked hard over his ears, arms out, his face pink, and with a fierce patter of "Come by, Come by, Whoa there lady, Come by!" sprints Backton's premier herdsman. He is actually quite impressive. Even without the farmyard he is theatrically convincing, and all the policeman can do is stand and stare in amazement as Farmer-Boy speeds past waving his old stick and shouting, *"They be chargin'! Stand back, stand back, the buggers'll trample 'ee!"* and disappears up the road.

I see Paddy's face in the back of the car. He's laughing again. A lot.

After all this, and Urge the Scurge spewing out the final fragments of Bad Religion's *Fuck Armageddon...This is Hell*, it would appear that the festival is finishing. People are beginning to disperse and the field looks suddenly full of litter. The stalls are packing up and the Cider Tent sign reads; "Closed – even for Rumpley's Scrumpy". With the atmosphere quietening down, the band offstage and the crowd departing, it seems unlikely there'll be any more trouble and I am beginning to let myself relax.

Then something else happens I didn't expect.

On the field's edge, not too far away, stands Muddy. He's on his own, still and quiet, his hands in his pockets, watching the people leave and the police moving the 'hoods' along. Then without warning, in one brisk, brief second, he takes out his hand and pitches a missile violently through the air. I don't know what it is, but it's small like a rock and it clips a policeman on the back of the leg. There is a shout as the policeman is hit. Then he turns, sees Muddy and flicks open a baton from his belt. Muddy, doubled over from the force of the baton, does not resist the arrest and is pulled roughly away to the cars. Again I'm thinking, "What on earth?" What on earth is going on? Bloody hell, the force of the baton! And the rock? Bloody hell, was Muddy's aim actually *meant* – I'm hoping, for his sake, it wasn't.

So it's another discomfiting conclusion. Well, almost a conclusion. The *real* ending, however, is Dave's.

As the noise of the afternoon melts away and the people disappear, his trenchant voice suddenly spikes the gathering dusk. He's yelling in a drunken drawl:

"It's *him*!" he slurs loudly. "*He's* the one you wanna talk to!"

Not content to stagger off with everybody else, Dave and Fat Uncle have fumbled onto the kiddies' ride. They are wedged together in one pink teacup, spinning round to the sound of *Mary, Mary, Quite Contrary*. The vendor is not happy and is shaking his fist, but the idiots ignore him.

"I said, *he's* the one!" shouts Dave. "Over there. *Him. Whatsisname!*" He's shrieking to the policemen up on the road, trying to grab their attention by waving an inflated condom in the air.

"It's *his* fault! It's *all* his fault. You wanna talk to *him*!" Dave points the condom over at me. "There he is look, *he's* your fuckin' man – *Whatsisname!*"

19

THE SIDE OF THE BANK

Not one little knick-knack had sold, at the festival. Not one delicate decoration.

"And Easter isn't far away. Surely *someone* needs a pastel-coloured tissue thing to hang up in the window. At Easter time. Surely."

True, people had looked at Sheryl's display – the ribbons and paper-crafts laid out carefully on her best, ironed tea towel. They'd even picked the tiny things up and looked at them with some interest. But like old fruit on a greengrocer's stall, the tiny things were unwanted and quickly placed back down.

"Honestly, decorations are always nice," thinks Sheryl. "Even as presents. And Christmas isn't far away. Well, nine months, but it soon flies by."

She packs the decorations away, returning them to the empty Walkers Crisps box she'd brought them in, trying not to crush the fine filigree and coloured beads.

"The festival is over anyway."

People are starting to leave, stumbling off with their pints of cider, slopping it over the sides, drifting home or somewhere else.

"They're not going to buy anything now. Might as well go home too."

Sheryl's thinking of a cup of tea – possibly a biscuit. There's half a packet of Super-Buy digestives in the kitchen cupboard. At least, there was a few days ago.

"Unless the kids have finished them off. Still, a cup of tea on its own, is good enough. Let's hope there's some milk left in the fridge."

She places a sequinned bauble gently in the box, between a hot-pink paper ruffle and a red serviette flower – some kind of rose maybe.

When the rock flies overhead and hits the policeman on the leg, Sheryl is smoothing the pale green tissue of a decoupage hummingbird. Then there's a kind of punching sound behind her, coupled with a shout as her fingertips touch the dainty wings; the fragile crispness of the paper as some way off across the field, the baton beats down on Muddy's neck.

It is with a sudden rashness that she throws the hummingbird in the box and the other knick-knacks on the top. Gathering up her belongings in a hasty armful, she trails urgently after the policeman and Muddy. By the time she reaches the road, however, the police car has already gone and she can only follow on foot – a small half-run, desperate and anxious, following the car to the station. It isn't quite what she'd planned for the afternoon, this panicky jog across the town after her miscreant son. A bit of income on the side maybe, cash in hand, tax-free etcetera, "And God knows we need it. But not this, we don't need *this*."

The knick-knacks are jumbled and squashed. It's awkward half-running carrying the box. Sheryl can't see where she's going. It's like coming down the stairs in the dark, cautiously feeling the next step, only she's breathless and het-up as well.

Twice she falls off the kerb and twists her knee, and once she bangs into a parked car.

At the dockside, the scuffing of her kitten heels echoes with the screech of the seagulls. The gulls are pushed inland by the wind, away from the sea to the riverbanks and rubbish tips. They're swooping down on the food-waste and chip paper in the scrubby grass. By the crumbling wall, one flaps too close to Sheryl, wings large and flapping hard in her face and, in fright, she misses her footing, slips through a gap in the barrier and slides down the side of the bank... just like that... over in a second... sliding down the bank. The wet clay and the sheer incline bring her straight down on her stomach, down through the bumps of mud and muck, fast, her breath knocked out – a skidding decline to the oily edge of the river. For a heartbeat Sheryl thinks; "I've not read any Tolstoy." Then she slides to a halt on an old bike wheel, and her skirt catches round the jutting spokes.

She stays still and breathes a while.

The mud is thick on her fingers and cold on her face, and it is with some difficulty she clutches at the clumps of scrubby grass, thin and razor-tipped, and pulls herself up slowly to the road. It certainly takes longer to climb back up than it did to slip-slide down.

When she's near the jagged concrete, and the yellow lines are level with her eyes, she searches around for the box that tilted from her arms as she fell. It is caught in some reeds, too far to reach, and the lids are hanging open at a slant, the ribbons and tissue stuff strewn in the mud.

Sheryl climbs up onto the road and looks down at the state of herself. There is seagull mess on her clothes, mixed in with

111

the mud. Her fingers are cut from the grass and she's lost a shoe in the clay. She can see it at the bottom of the bank; one little kitten-heel pointing up. She takes off her other shoe and begins to walk in bare feet, along the dirty pavement, staying close to the boarded shops. The pavement is uneven and hard underfoot and soon she is shivering.

Up on the bridge, people stare at this obviously gin-soaked madwoman, but Sheryl just stares out at the river, and the tiny green hummingbird bobbing on its side in the greasy brown scum below.

At the station, the police want her to stand on the mat by the open door. The seagull mess overpowers the smell of crime and illegal addiction, plus she's dropping mud on the station floor. She stands there for an hour and a half, rubbing her arms to keep warm and listening to the shouts from within. It's not Muddy, it's someone else. Muddy's quiet and eventually creeps out in silence, his head hanging and his hair round his face. In a confusion of relief and fury, Sheryl cuddles him like a child then kicks his backside all the way home. Poor Muddy, he skulks in front, his tall, skinny frame trying to dodge the aim of her bare foot.

On the main road nearing home, Sheryl, her feet sore from walking and kicking, stops for a moment to cool her soles on the base of a lamppost. It's then she realises three things: the sound of a woman calling her name; the sight of bars across the door of The Moon; and the feel of fresh dog mess between her toes.

The dog mess is moist.

The pub door is barred right up.

And the woman is poor old Olive.

Olive is the elderly lady for whom Sheryl shops just once a week: a bit of extra money on the side for taking round groceries, and 'looking out for'. Olive is across the road in her house and has pulled back the lace curtain at the front window. She's opened the window slightly – only slightly, for fear of air and letting in flies – and she's calling over to Sheryl: something about salad cream or shower gel. "Does Olive *shower*?" Sheryl can't make out her words, they're getting lost in the sound of car engines and the low exhaust pipes of the boy racers as they scrape full-tilt over the chicanes.

"Hang on Olive, I can't hear you!" shouts Sheryl.

Olive is waving her hand, feebly from the wrist.

"Wait a minute!" shouts Sheryl. "I'm coming!"

After wiping her foot uselessly on the pavement's edge, dislodging a small lump of excrement and smearing the rest across the back of her heel, Sheryl gives Muddy one last kick then heads over to Olive's house.

Olive is at the door now. The sound of the television blares out from somewhere beyond the dark hallway – *Eastenders* or *Emmerdale*.

"Come in, love," crackles Olive. "Can you get me some caustic soda? Sink's blocked again. Bloody thing."

"I won't come in, Olive. I'm a mess," replies Sheryl. "Caustic soda? *Again*?"

"Ooh, look at *you*." Olive's pale, rheumy eyes open wide. "What've you been up to? Playin' in mud I shouldn't wonder."

Sheryl hasn't played in mud since 1972 when she dug up worms on the allotment and threw them at her brother.

"Why's the sink blocked, Olive?"

Olive shrugs – her spindly shoulders poking through the seams of her cardigan.

"Olive, have you been tipping beef-fat down the plughole again?"

"No I haven't, darlin'. Not today."

"Olive, I've told you before, you mustn't tip beef-fat down the plughole. It blocks it up."

"Bollocks to that, darlin'."

"I'll fetch some soda in a minute. Get the plunger ready, and I'll sort it."

"Thank you darlin'." Olive shuts the door, and goes back to the window where she watches Sheryl up the road.

Bert, the manager of Super-Buy, is not too keen when Sheryl tiptoes in past the fresh veg he's just laid out. Not that anyone would buy veg. People are more into a tinned big breakfast than lipodene, "Or whatever it is that's in fresh tomatoes. Still, don't flick muck on them Sher, else there'll be *no* chance of shifting the buggers, and I've got 43 trays out the back going off."

Out the back, near the going-off tomatoes and the trolley cages and flattened boxes, Sheryl washes her feet in the metal sink and wipes the mud from her T-shirt and skirt. There are now even more patches of wet down her front, and her clothes are cold against her skin. She tries to dry them at the hand-dryer, but the air is barely warm and blows so weakly, it takes forever. So she unhitches her tabard from the peg and pulls it over her soiled hair, and clips the poppers at the waist – a cover-up job.

On the way out, when Bert's back is turned, she scoops up several tomatoes, finds a box of caustic soda (next to jam Swiss Roll for some odd reason) and heads back to poor old Olive.

As she crosses the road, Sheryl looks up again towards The Moon. There are no drinkers on the steps, or smokers, no dogs tied up outside, or babies left asleep in scruffy buggies. The pub is dead and barred. And the bars across the door are steel; five of them, thick and heavy and new, drilled in on either side, hard in the stone cladding and brick. A grubby little boy with nothing else to do, is striking a rhythm on the bars with an empty beer bottle, and up above his head where the pub sign used to hang, swings a pair of dirty boots.

Olive is pleased with the tomatoes. She puts them in the sideboard by the Crème de Menthe and talcum powder, and promptly forgets all about them.

In the kitchen, Sheryl cleans out the sink. She picks the detritus from the plughole; the slimy potato skins and bacon rind, the wet clumps of fluff matted together on thin strands of hair. It's all black and decomposing, smelling of sulphur or eggs, and the smell pervades the house.

Olive doesn't seem to notice the odour, having lived with it for a while. She's brought her nightdress down from upstairs and is busy getting ready for bed. She's nattering away in the front room, half to herself and half to Sheryl, pulling her old cardy off in the gloom as the stinking vapour wafts around.

"It'll be hard for you now, I expect," natters Olive. "It's hard for *everyone* now, what with them daft Eton Boys in Downin' Street. But it'll be harder for *you* now, I expect." Then to herself; "Bloody buttons, I can't do 'em."

"What's that?" replies Sheryl from the kitchen.

"I said, *'It'll be hard,'* – managin' and all that," says Olive. "You know, money-wise I mean." A cardigan button pings on the hearth. "Oh bugger it!"

Sheryl's not really listening. She's busy plunging the sink, and the beef-fat is floating back up.

"The Moon, Sher, The Moon," insists Olive. "'Tis closed."

"Oh Jesus, it stinks!"

"Too much fightin' and stuff. *Allegedly*. Where's me bed-socks? And illegal stuff: drugs and whatnot. Underage stuff as well. *Allegedly*."

Olive's pulling the old nightie over her head of thinning hair when Sheryl comes in from the back. There's beef-fat down her tabard, and she's carrying the plunger.

"'Tis closed, Sher," says Olive, fumbling with the winceyette collar.

Sheryl's staring, confused.

"*The Moon*," says Olive. "Closed. Not just for today." She pronounces the next words precisely, in the way she overheard the police; "Closed for the *foreseeable future*. Did you do the sink?"

"What? Oh, yes, it's done. Olive, you mustn't tip beef-fat down the plughole, OK?"

"OK darlin'. Do you want some money?"

"No Olive, of course not. I only unblocked the sink."

"To tide you over I mean, now you lost your job at The Moon. I got savin's in the Post Office. You're welcome to have some darlin'."

Sheryl thinks Olive's a sweetie, but she doesn't take the money. She helps the old lady brush her hair then she takes her up to bed and tucks her in for the night.

Olive grins up at her from the pillow. "Darlin', are you goin' to San Francisco?"

"Am I going *where*?"

"You got bare feet, like a hippy."

Sheryl sighs. "No Olive, I'm not going to San Francisco. Have you got your bed-socks on?"

"No, bloody things have gone."

Sheryl finds the bed-socks (in the fridge, by Olive's spectacles) then takes them back upstairs and ruches them on Olive's feet. Her feet are grey and swollen as she pokes them out from the eiderdown, and her bed smells sour and unwashed.

"I'll change your sheets tomorrow, if you like," offers Sheryl.

"Thank you darlin'. You're so kind." Then Olive whispers; "You should've been a nurse."

Sheryl smiles a little.

Then Olive mutters; "But you stink of bird-shit."

"Goodnight Olive."

"Goodnight darlin'."

Muddy is in the garage when Sheryl finally arrives back home. He's sitting in the dark with his guitar, strumming a minor chord over and over again. It's a low sound of manic repetition, and when Sheryl grates open the door and offers to fry him some chips, he shakes his head in time to the rhythm – compulsive and empty.

Sheryl goes back inside and rests against the kitchen unit as the kettle comes to the boil. Her feet ache and the skin on her left shin is cut, and she's so tired, she can barely find the energy to pour the cup of black tea – no milk left after all.

In the front room, the dim glow from the broken lampshade shows the dust on the television and the bars of the electric fire. It's a small pool of light that just touches the corners of her old books and the worn-white edges of their paper jackets as they lean in an upright line against the wall. Running her fingers along the spines, Sheryl takes a book out and stares at the cover. It's a picture she remembers from '75, that each time she sees it, conjures old jumble sales and grey skies, and snow so deep it came past the downstairs windows. She'd curled herself in a chair and begun to read, as the snow grew higher outside, and her father dug a path from the door.

Sheryl turns out the broken light and goes upstairs to bed, underneath the covers with an Ever-Ready torch.

And as the traffic sounds steal in from the main road, and the past day flickers in her head, Sheryl turns the page of *On the Banks of Plum Creek* and reads once again the first lines of Laura Ingalls-Wilder.

20

DIARY – FROM TENNESSEE TO THE INFIRMARY

Special Measures.

We are in them: this bricked-up, asbestos-clad institution.

It's front page, local news; a worldwide declaration of direness.

'That Place':

Failing.

On all counts.

Nearly.

Apart from the management structure which, apparently, is satisfactory.

I wonder what Special Measures will be taken: the removal of biscuits from the Head's office? More stationery catalogues for Resources? An extra Truant Officer to slap a fine of a thousand pounds on the single parents of absent children? The answers to all the problems are endless!

In the school, I weave my way through the mass of pupils forced to work in the main corridor whilst the rainwater drips from the ceilings of their classrooms into buckets. The teachers are white-eyed and shouty.

In the lab, I take my *own* Special Measures; a basic, knee-jerk, pop-up book reaction when a kid picks up a stool and throws it. Why don't they nail the stools down?

He is bigger than me, with the first shade of a moustache, and an angry, jutting brow. He is too old for school, he says. At 14, the future is in taking cars. Obviously from town, not outside: he's never left the town; never been to the beach or the hills for a day-trip; only the streets. He has no books and little uniform, just a white shirt and combat trousers, and a dog-chain from the waist. He is not happy where I ask him to sit (near the front, at the side), and he is not going to sit on the stool. He is, however, going to chuck it at my face. Another kid, a smaller boy, suddenly intervenes. He suffers with notable anxiety, and is shaky, trying to be brave. He goes to grab the bigger boy's chain to pull him back, but luckily he misses and *I* get the stool instead.

I don't need this anymore.

I walk out. Along the busy corridor to the Head of Year, and say: "I don't need this anymore. *You* deal with it."

And I leave.

Walk out, with the brazenfaced truants out the front door.

I have no idea what happened to the class.

Amazingly, I still have a job. Just. Though I'm not there the rest of today, or tomorrow, or the next. I'm here, by the docks, experiencing in their words 'emotional space'.

How ironic: 'emotional space' by the dockside wall as it crumbles away to the riverbed, as it deteriorates back to the Neolithic age, and nothing.

So I'm staring at the rubble and the scrub grass, and the seagulls as they bob on the slick, whilst through the open door of the radio shop, they discuss my case.

"You should've punched him!" booms Frankie from inside. "Punched his lights out. What a tosser!" She pauses as the wirelesses announce; "*And that were our local favourites again, Urge the Scurge, currently on bail for criminal damage to a police car. Next up, Beyonce, not on bail for criminal damage.*"

When Taser mentions his friend, I'm gazing down at the mud and a small pink shoe, vibrant against the dull colours of the bank. Its heel is pointing up in the air.

Taser is standing in the door of the shop which, given the rapid decay of the wall, is now only ten feet from the brink of the river and the little pink shoe below.

"Well, I guess I know Kaz Beeblosa," he says vaguely, rummaging noisily in a big plastic bag.

Silt slides against the upturned shoe.

"Kaz who?" I ask sharply.

"Kaz Beeblosa. You know? That drummer?"

"Yes, I know who Kaz Beeblosa is," I snap, spinning round to face him. "What do you mean, you *know* him?"

"He slept on my floor once, couple o' year ago," he replies innocently through mouthfuls of cheese and onion pasty.

The seagulls screech into the sky as I stare in amazement at Taser's gormless expression.

"When I lived in Woodspring Grove," he says, absently.

Frankie interrupts from inside the shop; "*God, that were an awful dive, that were!*" she shouts. "*Brand new Boofer home on the gingerbread estate. Paper walls and stuff!*"

"*Yep, and a bloody long walk into town on a Friday night!*" shouts back Taser.

"*Why didn't you catch the bus?*" calls Frankie.

"*I dunno!*" calls back Taser.

121

What on earth are they doing? They're yabbering on about buses and Boofer homes when Taser has just revealed possibly the single most important, fundamentally crucial piece of information I need for the future of music promotion.

Taser knows Kaz Beeblosa?

Kaz Beeblosa's slept on Taser's floor?

It's the equivalent of a Soviet-state secret being released in Washington D.C. ...or Backton.

This sings and rings of good fortune, for the fat bloater Kaz Beeblosa is the drummer in Shooting Horses – an 'almost there' rock band charging in from Tennessee to the lower reaches of the UK chart. I don't ask the background to Taser's mysterious circumstances: I don't care. The dollar signs are ker-chinging in my eyes.

And Taser knows Kaz's number – surprisingly, by heart!

"Course I know his number. He still owes me 15 quid for a broken toilet seat!"

I don't mention the toilet seat when I chat to Kaz Beeblosa. It's 7am in Tennessee, and he's not exactly burning with delight to be woken up by a neurotic, hysterical Englishman. It's a distinct, Southern-American, hung-over drawl, winding through a knotted beard; "Man, are you a goddam, fuckin' lady-boy? 'Cos you sure are screamin' down the phone. Not that I give a she-it. Some of my best friends take it up the ay-ass."

No, definitely won't mention the toilet seat. Nevertheless, I *do* mention Taser and Backton, and Kaz remembers them both. But, despite these two potential drawbacks, he agrees immediately to a gig. I can't believe it. He says a fee. I agree. It's done. Three weeks on Saturday. I can't believe it. Then I lie about the venue: because I haven't got one; and because Kaz is used to playing concert-tour academies across Europe and North America – not a room above a pub in town.

As I say, I lie about the venue.

Oh God, the venue?

The back door of The Infirmary nightclub is midnight blue. From the outside, it blends into the midnight blue walls, almost replete with posters of forthcoming events. The posters are coming unstuck, and their corners flap in the vicious breeze. As I knock on the door for attention, one of the posters rips off from the wall, and as I stoop to pick it up, the door opens and a thickset man steps out.

"Do you mind not pulling down my gear," he growls, snatching the poster from my hand. He looks down at the advert in his brawny fist and sees a picture of a woman gyrating in a bra and mini-skirt, together with the words: "*Ladies, free-entry, Thursdays.*"

He stares nastily in my face. "We get a lot of young blokes like *you* on Thursdays."

What does he mean "like *me*"?

As I fear his explanation, I move on. "Hi, you must be Cedric. I'm Martin. Pleased to meet you."

"Really," he says, unimpressed by my light vivacity. "The Infirmary doesn't come cheap mate, I'll tell you that for nothin'."

He shows me inside and bangs the door behind. He doesn't take his piggy eyes off me for one second, glaring malevolently as he slams down the fire-bar in a single powerful jab from one hand. Silently, he shoos me through the club, and I scuttle along like a poodle.

Cedric, the chief bouncer, wears a weight-lifting belt and walks like a body-builder, his muscular arms held out from his side. His neck is wide and shaven, as is his head. Scuttling along, I lose my sense of direction; the corridors of The Infirmary are windowless and dim, but Cedric knows the narrow passages like the back of his Grizzly-Bear paw, and soon we arrive in a small fluorescent-lit office.

It's cramped and not particularly welcoming in the office, with a large iron safe bolted into the floor, and a dozen crates containing bottles of whiskey stacked against the plywood wall. Sitting behind the scruffy desk, Hugo, The Infirmary owner, flicks through estate agents' property details. In front of him, spread out in serried rows, are thick wadges of 20 pound notes all trussed up in red rubber bands. I've never seen so much money in my life, and Cedric catches me gazing.

"Oi! Keep yer mitts off, mate!" he barks. Then he points close up to my nose, and just stares.

Almost as if Cedric hasn't spoken, Hugo rises from the chair and, with a genial authority, walks towards me and extends a hand.

"Hi there. Hugo Freudenberg. Thanks a lot for popping in, Martin. Take a seat."

His handshake is brief, firm and flaunts an antique Rolex on the wrist. The difference from Cedric is astonishing. And relieving. Hugo is young, about 30, and friendly, well spoken, with a confident public-school air and the brown brogues of an apparently well-heeled businessman. Unlike Cedric, he is warm, professional and enthusiastic and it's clear he likes my ideas. Whilst Cedric skulks by the door, Hugo suggests plans and possibilities, development, publicity and strategy. With an immediate eye for commercial detail, he disseminates the facts and figures quickly, and by the end of the meeting, we have a pro-forma contract drawn up and the basis of a bargain; a two-way split on ticket sales, plus The Infirmary has the profits on the bar.

At this point, Cedric, hitherto a heavy-breathing presence in the background, leans in and says in my ear; "That's a fuckin' good deal, mate. I'd chew my own bollocks off for that."

Quite.

Giving a polite request to collect his car, and specific instructions to mind the paintwork, Hugo hands Cedric a large bunch of keys, and Cedric strides off. Then Hugo leads me back through the dark to the main bar.

"We should get 700 in here, no problem," he says, stepping up onto the half-lit dance-floor. The steel tips of his brogues clip purposefully on the laminate tiles. "And we'll open the back bar as well, get another 300 in there. Should be fine. What do *you* think?"

What do *I* think?

My trainers make a babyish shuffling sound.

Thousands of pounds are at stake.

The dance-floor looks cavernous, the ceilings too high, the stage like a six-lane motorway. I'm breathing in the stale beer and the distant smell of men's toilets, Cedric's hairy knuckles are worryingly at the back of my mind.

What do *I* think?

"Absolutely. Should be fine."

This time I'm shown the *front* door.

Outside, the wind still whips, gusting up whirlwinds of grey dust. As I stand on the pavement, I can't help wondering if I've made the right decision. Not only does the club seem vast, too vast for me to fill, will people *want* to come? This part of town is largely squalid and ugly. No real future or attempt to invest, unless it's as a pocket-sized sweetener from a bull-dozing corporate chain. Is the gig enough to attract a crowd here? Will people *want* to come? I glance up at The Infirmary façade, with its pale gold angular lamps slowly brightening in the late afternoon gloom. They glow from the eaves and upper windowsills like geometric sunbursts. A way back, before Hugo came to the rescue, The Infirmary was derelict and threatened with demolition. From here, it's a beautiful Art-Deco building, once the hospital to the town. It's symmetrical, with structural lines and a feeling of period opulence, whilst its neighbours on either side are, in comparison, shabby and modernised and somehow inappropriate – the gaudy fancy-dress hire, and the frugal display of the funeral director. Will people *want* to come?

I walk away. I have a headful of Baby Dolls and holy bibles, disco floors and doubts. Then, from up the wind-dusted street, blasts the car-horn. It's loud and insistent and accompanied by shouting. A second later, a vehicle revs into view. It's driven fast and erratically, twisting through the rubbish, a vintage maroon Mini with a T-Cut shine and silver wing mirrors. And crammed into the front seat, his crew-cut pressing the roof and his muscular build bulging both doors, is Cedric. His face is puce, and his piggy eyes wild, and the front bumper is caved right in.

21

Aran's Christmas Eve

The supermarket is the work of the devil: a ruinous corruption causing suffering and sin. All seven of the sins in fact, and Aran knows the name of each: lust, gluttony, avarice, sloth, wrath, envy and pride.

They are in the aisles, all of them, heavy and oppressive, smogging the air with their emotional intensity so Aran cannot breathe. He finds it truly unbearable – the claustrophobic impiety in the unending shelves of food; eat and eat and eat, over and over again. He finds it morally repugnant – the lazy, lumpen flesh of the obese and the weight of their un-steerable trolleys filled with carbohydrate bulk. And he's suffocated by the rage of the checkout queue and the wallets stuffed with credit and loyalty cards and money loaned from the Cash Converter.

So Aran stays at home; inside, on his own, on a high stool in the hallway, waiting for the knock at the door and his shopping to be delivered. Sitting on his own: in the hallway, with its stairs and bannisters and carpet-edges and doorway boundary-lines. Waiting.

As he waits, Aran thanks the Holy Spirit for his own breath, and the peace, and the sight of Taser's back as he'd left with his plastic bag, down the path – *finally*. Because that lodger had been a mistake: more money, yes, and no effort, but with it, avarice and sloth and the degradation of the soul.

Things are tidier like this – alone. Ordered and controlled. Things are put away in boxes and cupboards and compartments. Tucked away. Unacknowledged.

When the knock at the door raps out in the silence of the hall, Aran doesn't jump. He rises slowly from the stool, turns the key in the lock and opens the door just a fingerbreadth. He signs his name for the groceries by reaching through the gap with his skinny wrist: a tiny, compressed, barely-visible signature, written with care and precision, but not speed. Then he closes the door, leaving the groceries outside and goes to the bathroom and washes his hands – it wasn't *his* pen with which he'd signed.

The groceries fill two cartons and almost match his requirements. He had originally requested chocolate; milk chocolate in miniature squares, but receives a 60-watt light bulb instead. The rest appears to be per the list:

Disinfectant
Carpet cleaner
Bleach.
Jelly babies
Dolly Mixtures
Gum.
Lemonade pop
10 cigarettes

And drink: a variety of nice stuff, sweet and bright – cherry-red kirsch and orange liquor, a bottle of blue curacao.

He sets out each item on the kitchen unit, one beside the other, equidistant in between, and ticks them off his list. Then he separates the chemicals from the consumables, and methodically begins to clean; in every room, on every surface, the same spot six times over, till the tops shine like still mill-pools, and the hoover lines up the carpet-pile like the stripes on a well-mown lawn.

Aran almost sings as he follows his routine, from the attic door to the back door – a contented, under-the-breath tune in a series of quiet, light notes. It is a happiness regained from once before, and this is almost as it was once before. What a relief to claim back his space and create the rules again. And this time he would play the game to *his* rules, *properly*: he wouldn't lose or be stupid, he wouldn't get caught – a collared con and felon.

The grit and dust are brushed away, the dead skin-cells and the grime, to make way for more; layer upon layer of more dirt, the filth of the future. But Aran knows it can be scoured again: once cleaned, easier to keep clean. It's a scientific fact, though science has no place in His plan. And God knows cleanliness is next to godliness. It's the air Aran cannot cleanse – the exosphere and chemosphere, and the dirt that punctures the ether in sound waves, vibrations and energies. But put that away in the boxes and cupboards and compartments at the back of the mind. Tucked away. Unacknowledged.

When the last of the surfaces is wiped, Aran takes the consumables and arranges them precisely, on the nest of tables in the sitting room. It is important to perfect this arrangement for maximum effect; it's part of the game. So he conjures a tiered, carefully constructed pyramid of colour and flavour. The sweets and lemonade and brightly luminous drink, enticing and captivating, like the window of an old-fashioned confectioners. It is a display to be admired. One should take the time to appeal to the discerning customer, however young one hopes they might be, not shove everything out on a gondola-aisle for the very general public; a 'buy one, get one free' flab of doughnuts sweating under the strip-lights.

Aran feels the need to sit and venerate his work, but the cat is here curled in the armchair, flexing claws and louring. So he carries in the stool from the hall, places it close by his arrangement, and sits and stares. It is exciting, nerve tingling. Like Christmas might've been if they'd ever hung a stocking up and sung carols around a tree. Looking forward and hoping.

Like Christmas Eve.

Probably.

22

Diary – Kaz Beeblosa Comes to Town

Chopper bikes.

Dr. Marten's.

Pink Floyd's coloured prism.

Iconic.

And I'm in it – Hugo's vintage Mini.

It's mini and goes like a bomb. Or at least, it feels it does. Or maybe that's my arse so close to the ground. It must look pretty good on the outside (the Mini, not my arse), cutting round corners and nipping in spaces, and it looks pretty good on the *inside*; the seats are leather, the gearstick's mahogany, and the steering wheel would fit a bus. And it's me driving, with my eye on the massive speedometer, and my elbow out the sliding window. I want this car. I'd want it even more if I weren't fretting about other things – tonight, for example.

I'm driving to the station, the small two-platform station on the outskirts of town, to collect Kaz Beeblosa from the train. My own car is out of action having developed an electrical fault, which means I can't open any of the doors. No problems with the Mini doors though. No central locking or NASA-style super-technology to keep you out.

When I swerve into the station, Kaz is already waiting. He's standing on the pavement in the midday sunshine, looking up the road for the next car to come along. Somehow I get the feeling he wasn't expecting the Mini, or something quite so small. And to be honest, I wasn't really expecting Kaz to be quite so big. I mean, I always knew he was *big*, just not *this* big. If this is reality (and I'm beginning to hope it isn't), then TV must've warped the perspective, for horizontally he seems to have expanded, and vertically he seems to have contracted, like 'Potty-Putty' in the school lab.

Size-ist.
Mustn't be size-ist.
It's just the bloody car that's suddenly a problem.
Professional.
Must be professional.

I ignore the images lumbering in my head, of large people in freak-show documentaries, being winched from their houses by cranes, and I become instead, a gushing, sycophantic fool.

"Kaz! Hi there! It's *wonderful* to meet you. Thank you *so much* for coming. Welcome back to Backton. Oh! '*Back to Backton*' – sounds like the name of a song!"

Kaz flinches as if interrupted by a persistent gnat, and whips his beard round to face me. Then he growls:

"Are you the goddam, fuckin' lady-boy?"

"Umm...yes. Yes, I am. Martin Price, pleased to meet you."

Kaz is glaring at the Mini. "You gotta be fuckin' kiddin' me, right?"

"Umm..."

132

"How, in the name of all that's goddam sane, are we gonna carry *this* she-it?" Kaz takes a step to the side to reveal behind him the biggest roundest drum-case I have ever seen – surprisingly, up till now, concealed by the shape of his body. Just in time, I manage to stop myself from bleating, "How did I not see *that*?" and just say weakly, "It's not small, is it?"

Kaz is threateningly silent as we push the drum-case onto the roof and tie it down with a couple of bunjees I've found in the boot. When he gets in the seat, the Mini lurches ominously to one side and I hear the drum-case move above. Even more awkward is the fact Kaz is too large for the belt and has to hold it round himself with one hand, whilst the other hand holds onto the door, which cannot shut for the overspill of flesh.

I drive off slowly and stay in first gear – I cannot change to second for the pressure of his thigh.

A little way down the road, Kaz barks; "You gotta Walmart?"

"...Pardon?...Have I got a *wall*?"

"Jesus man, I'm not askin' if you gotta *wall*, and I'm not callin' you *Mart*. I'm askin' if you gotta *Walmart*."

Is it me, or is this not going well?

I chug Kaz along to Asda.

Stardom.

Glory.

Celebrity.

Because of these, something happens in the shop: something profound to Kaz's demeanour. We're selecting the special-offer doughnuts, perusing the beef and onion pasties, mulling over banana milk, then stacking up on the Jack Daniels and rum. I pay for this sickly rider (requested by Kaz) whilst he kicks up a fame-furore in the biscuit aisle: he's loving the attention that's stalking him around – the squeals of excitement, and the lip-gloss kisses as sticky and sweet as the filling in a fig-roll. And all of a sudden he's gone – the barking, snarling rocker – and in his place, a warm, charismatic, chivalrous knight; one who signs autographs on damsels' breasts.

When we leave, we're waved off! And as we chug out past the recycling skips and the broken beer bottles, and the waste paper flying in the air, Kaz purrs; "I *love* this city."

23

ARAN TAKES HIS SHARE

Aran picks his way through the town, through the littered shortcuts and alleys. He keeps away from the main roads, the traffic and the staring motorists – away from the danger and the prying looks. He keeps instead to the side streets, creeping past the tenements that gaze dully on the shop-backs and the delivery doors and bins. It's the soiled pavements he's following, with their ground-down chewing-gum stains, those pavements in the little streets too narrow for the road-cleaning lorry. He picks his way delicately, tip-toeing to avoid the dirt. And his expression is cold, his mouth is hard and he's focussed, fixed, monomaniac.

When he reaches the side-gate to the park, his breathing is rapid and short, and he's thinking to the beat of his heart:

The game;

With sweets,

And drink.

To play.

To sit.

To wait.

In the sunshine, people close their eyes. They rest, get lazy, don't watch, don't listen. It's appalling, the feats of audacity that can be accomplished when a back is turned, when the eye is taken off the ball for a short while.

Aran decides to pause, to make sure the back *is* turned, and his presence so far unnoticed. It's important to perfect this invisibility for maximum effect; it's part of the game. So he stays still momentarily by the gate and assesses the situation, pausing and observing the people as they lie in the last of the sun. They're happy and indolent with their cigarettes, and he thinks again to the beat of his heart:

Don't look.

Don't hear.

No collared con.

I'll take.

You'll give.

I'll win.

There is order in the rhythm of his heart, an order that points his concentration, steels his nerve and fires his gut. Aran likes it; it matches the sense of system in his plan, the structure in his rules, and the rules are:

I'll take, you'll give, I'll win, you'll lose.

Order, system and structure: carefully constructed rules that will crumble into moral decay and disarray.

Aran assesses the situation.

In the sunshine, people close their eyes. They rest, get lazy, don't watch, don't listen. It's appalling, the feats of audacity that can be accomplished when a back is turned, when the eye is taken off the ball for a short while.

Pay attention!

Attention will be paid too late.

Aran knows he won't get caught this time, for his plan is

going to plan. He will be allowed and permitted to get what he wants, illegitimate hopes fully realised with no fear of legal repercussions. He almost sings as he follows his plan, from the gate of the park to the shade of the trees – a contented, under-the-breath tune in a series of quiet, light notes. It is a happiness regained from once before, and this is almost as it was once before.

From the shade of the trees, to the grass of the park, see the bright, fresh glow of white skin ignored in the warmth of the day.

Pay attention!

Attention will be paid too late.

Aran thinks to the beat of his heart:

Anger.

Envy.

And losing out.

To play.

To take.

Back home.

This time, he is absolutely certain: he is going to take his share: a nice big piece of the pie. Again: another little hand in his.

24

DIARY – WHO'S THAT GUY?

Sound-check.

The Infirmary.

And Kaz's demeanour has reverted.

"One. Two. One. Two," Kaz is growling. "One. Two. One. Two. Three men. Two men. Acumen! You gotta whole lotta business acumen! Bitumen! I wanna hot tub full o' bitumen!"

I think Kaz might be bored.

"Abdomen! I gotta super-size, six-man abdomen!"

He's rapping the sound-check. Sitting monster-like behind the drum-kit, banging the bass drum on a steady, repetitious beat and growling grim drivel into the mic.

"Albumen! I wanna wipe yer face in albumen!"

Yep. He *is* bored. Even his beard looks bored. It hangs in a dejected, twisted lank. As he raps, Kaz glowers at me over the rim of a cymbal, staring with a fierce, steady gaze. It is clear he regards me with contempt, as an incompetent loon with all the professionalism of cheese.

I am standing alongside him onstage, wearing the guitarist's Stratocaster: because the guitarist is still not here. Where is he? No-one knows. He's somewhere, obviously, but that somewhere is a point anywhere between Tennessee and

Backton. So I'm standing, and nervously strumming an 'F' chord (out of time) and thinking the 'F' word, because if I have to stand in for bloody Slash or whoever it is, I will just have a total meltdown.

Kaz is still glowering at me. "Specimen! You're gonna give a yellow-green, Brit-piss specimen!"

Oh God.

When the sound-check is over, my palms are sweating, but my heart is singing; hymns of praise to the Lord. Thank the Lord that's over.

The bassist and the lead singer decide to head off for a break. The bassist, a willowy woman called Jo-Beth, has an unusual style of playing – aggressively provocative like Dee Dee Ramone crossed with a D-cup lap-dancer – whilst the lead singer, Simian, is friendly, twinkly, and camp beyond any quantifiable measure. He is wearing skin-tight Lycra trousers with a monochrome cock and ball print. Before the gig, Simian and Jo-Beth want to experience the "full-frontal fun of the seething Backton nightlife". I don't comment on their inappropriate use of the words "nightlife", and "fun", but direct them instead to a nearby pub. I add the warning that the Lycra trousers may not inspire immediate cordial relations, but they're not bothered about that, in fact they seem pleased.

Kaz, Hugo, the sound-guy and I go upstairs to the bar and sit down to a take-out meal I ordered earlier. It's a buffet, and Kaz is less than impressed.

"What the fuck is this she-it?" He plucks up a Ritz cracker and pops it in the midst of his beard. The cracker disappears and Kaz chews for a moment. Then he snaps; "Jesus, Martin, I'm not Karen goddam Carpenter, I want some *food* for Christ sakes!" Hugo pours him a Jack Daniels, makes a phone call and within ten minutes, Cedric appears with lamb shanks in barbecue sauce and a ton of spare ribs on the side. He places the tray delicately down on the table, then fetches some gleaming cutlery from behind the bar, takes a cotton napkin and shakes it out and, like an efficient barber at the start of a shave, ties it snugly around Kaz's thick neck. I watch, surprised at Cedric's quiet obedience and deference. As he slips away, he passes by my side and whispers: "Get it right you prat. If Mr. Beeblosa so desires it, it shall be done."

Kaz and the sound-guy pitch in to the food, as does another guy who's just turned up, sidling in and sitting with us. He's middle-aged and beery-breathed with unwashed hair and unwashed clothes, but apparently knows Kaz and the sound-guy, leering along with their jokes, and nudging their elbows with his. Before long, they're all swapping stories of life on the road, and Kaz is mellowing as the whiskey slips down. It's a pleasant, convivial atmosphere with tall tales of beaten-up cadillacs, and hookers from the wrong side of the tracks. Hugo is relaxed and confident, joining in with the repartee, and Kaz is loving his cut-glass accent and his anecdotes of Backton and The Infirmary.

"You should come over to the city, Hugo," says Kaz. "Come over to my place. Tennessee if you want. Or California. I got an apartment out on the coast. It's fuckin' 'A', man."

Bloody hell, an invite to California from Kaz Beeblosa! I wait expectantly for Kaz to look *my* way.

But he doesn't.

Hugo pours him another drink, and 'the guy who's just turned up' tells a lewd joke and they all laugh. Then there's the sound of high heels on the stairs and Simian and Jo-Beth return. It transpires they have not only been barred entry from the first pub, but several others along the way, as well as a newsagent's, a chemist's and the Pound Shop (late night shopping on a Saturday evening). I don't quite know what to say, but they look delighted by the disconcertion they've raised and celebrate with a Manhattan cocktail. I wish *I* could mix a cocktail like Hugo, with a disaffected nonchalance and style. Hugo pours me one like the others', and proposes an impromptu toast.

"To Martin Price Music Promotion, and to the gig – may she be a good one!"

Everyone raises a glass, then 'the guy who's just turned up' makes short work of the last lamb shank, gulps a whiskey, and disappears.

Kaz is sleepy now, so I show him to the B&B for a pre-gig rest. It's a 17th century inn, on the next street along, in the oldest part of town – not far at all and not worth the car, but a distance for Kaz who's tired and heavy on his feet. We walk slowly and, as we've little conversation, I decide to enquire after 'the guy who'd just turned up'.

"Kaz, who was the guy who just turned up, not the sound-guy, the other guy, you know, your friend?"

Kaz stops for a moment, breathing heavily, looks around in bewilderment, and peers at me confused. Then he drawls; "How…the hay'll…should I know!"

25

THE LONG WALK BACK TO POUND STREET

Bruce has received two letters, and both are unexpected. He found them on the doormat this morning, amongst the "no-win, no-fee" insurance offers, and the money-off coupons at Iceland (pizza and arctic roll).

The letters are conspicuous by their formality – Mr. B. Boonsby esq., – and by their crisp white envelopes, and postmarks; one local, one Spanish.

Bruce doesn't like the look of either letter, but especially the one from Spain, and as he tears the envelope open, he has a sudden twisting of his stomach.

It must be Susan.

Or about Susan.

It must be.

What's happened?

Has something happened?

It's Susan. Making contact. After so long: so many years. It's *her* name on the letter: in bold print. Making contact officially, through a third party.

Bruce sits on the chair, by the door. He had assumed it was *bad* news, had hoped it was *good* news, and now discovers it's neither.

Susan has found a loophole (something to do with the false establishment of the settlement) and has instructed a feral solicitor.

The letter is brittle, precise, and leaves him hollow, feeling precisely nothing. He'd hoped too much for the good news, and it's clear now that his hope was ridiculous and also totally unfounded:

Susan is *not* coming home.

The other letter, the local postmark, is a photocopied, standardised reply to a recent job application. It's as brittle as the Spanish letter and as ultimately hopeless – a Dear John, thanks-but-no-thanks. Well, at least they'd bothered to reply.

Bruce drinks tea, and thinks; empty, idle thoughts. Then walks. He walks the streets of Backton. From his doorstep in Pound Street, through town to the park and the children playing, past the factory and the chimney remains. Everywhere. Anywhere. There's no aim or focus to walking, just walking for the sake of walking. Anywhere.

By late afternoon, his empty thoughts have turned, with the winding of the streets, to a final destination: the boy on the factory floor. Bruce wonders at 'hope' and, if allowed, the terrible, remote places to which it can drive you. And he wonders at the little minor roads of faith along the way that, if you're lucky, draw you in, keep you safe and lead you home.

He passes the fancy-dress hire and the funeral director's and arrives at the beautiful Infirmary. For a second he hesitates, undecided whether to stay and go in, then reconsiders and carries on, along the street, through the old part of town with its huddle-roofed buildings and cobbles, and so to the Community Club. He looks through the open door, beyond the long passage to the bar. The stool is on the stage, and nearby on the velour sofa, Rosie sits waiting patiently, her mother's wheelchair by her side.

Bruce wonders at 'hope', and the minor roads of faith, and then takes the long walk back to Pound Street and what once was Susan's house.

In the sitting room, by the bookshelf, as always rests his guitar, ready to play tonight the Mid-West ballads and soft-shoe shuffles and the songs of love and heartbreak; the realities of life. It makes a tuneless, empty sound as he removes the fraying strap, and resonates behind him as he drags the strap upstairs to the attic, and the rafters up above.

26

Diary – The 'F' Chord Diminished

Kaz is sprawled out on his bed in the B&B, staring up at the sloping roof and the rough black beams that cross overhead. His great round stomach protrudes in the air, rising and falling with every breath, and from where I'm standing, by the door, his gut hides his face from view.

He drawls asthmatically; "How old d'you say this place is?"

I actually have no idea, but not wanting to appear more stupid than Kaz already thinks I am, I tell him it's 17th century. Then I add for dramatic effect; "It used to be a friary... Franciscan... and...er...Benedictine."

There's a long suspicious silence followed by the sound of my voice uttering the words "headless", "monk" and "murder." As soon as I stop talking, I think; "*Why?*"

There's a pause in the stomach-rise as Kaz reflects thoughtfully on my daft and historically inaccurate point of interest.

"Jesus, man...this place is so...*old*."

He wheezes for a bit and then asks; "Can you pass me the J.D.?"

I fetch the bottle from his bag and he lumbers up on to his

elbow, takes a hefty swig and lies back down again. I wait for a moment for further instruction, but with none forthcoming, say decisively: "Right then. 8 pm start, OK?"

But Kaz does not respond. He's snoring gently now, and his stomach continues to rise and fall with each laboured intake of breath.

There's a slight tension at The Infirmary when I return. The guitarist has still not arrived and I gather, from overheard, hushed conversations, that Jo-Beth, Simian and the sound-guy would rather stab themselves repeatedly with a tuning fork than have me as an onstage replacement. I couldn't agree more. However, since nobody can ascertain the whereabouts of Slash-or-whoever-it-is, my next role as so-called 'promoter' is the one I was dreading most. The chords are handed to me reluctantly, and in readiness, scrawled on a selection of beer mats.

Bruce Boonsby, I need your advice.

I'm in a dark corner, literally and perhaps metaphorically: hidden away in a small room off another small room, wondering at the course of events and whether Harvey Goldsmith ever found himself in a similar position; trying to play an 'F' chord diminished, in a small room off another small room, in a small town, for a band he's only just met.

Possibly?

No.

The fumbling practice lasts an hour, which passes like a minute, and culminates in a 'B' flat, three blisters, and a banging on the back door.

It's Kaz.

He's back, and standing in the gloom, soaking wet, white-eyed and muttering. Slightly puzzled, I enquire how he slept, but Kaz just makes a weird guttural noise, and before I can work it out, Cedric hoves into view unexpectedly, like an Eddie Stobart lorry in a country lane; rumbling and large. He barges past us, hissing through his teeth and forcing us along the corridor. As Cedric sweeps us up to the stage, Kaz moves closer behind me. I can definitely feel his gut, and I can almost feel the grating edge of his growl. He's snarling something about a sudden cold breeze, a headless monk, and how he's going to bust my butt for putting him up in a "fuckin' church" with only a litre of Jack Daniels to keep him company.

Kaz is freaked out. As he forces his bulk behind the drums, his eyes are dilated and savage, and he grips the drumsticks like a butcher with two meat-cleavers. Drips are running from the tip of his beard, over the swell of his stomach, and for a second, he catches me staring; "And it's goddam fuckin' *rainin'*, boy!" he screams.

I think it's fair to say, it is yet another kind of nightmare in which I'm now pivoting, as the almighty crowd cheers and the cleavers smash down. It is a bad dream of anger, confusion and fear, and the rushing of blood in my ears. I am four bars in, and my fingers won't move, like leaden limbs struggling from the pursuit of torment. If I spoke, would there be any sound? Would anyone hear me? If I fell, would I hit the ground? I am woken only by a tall leather-clad figure before me, emerging from the front row, up on to the stage, and lifting the guitar over my head. There are screams of delight and stamping from the

147

crowd as the blessed 'F' diminished rings out, powerful and strong to the roof and the clouds and the heavenly angels beyond.

Good Fortune.
Faith.
It is the sweetest of dawns, at last.
He is here:
Slash-or-whoever-it-is.
Our saviour!

27

THE MINOR ROAD

Down by the river, mid-town, where the water shifts as thick as cement, slips Backton Docks. By the broken dockside wall and its crumbling blue lias, declines the future. For the boarded shops and Georgian flats are hesitating on feeble foundations. Bricks and mortar are becoming the past, and so too, prosperity and prospects.

Now life is poorer.

Once more, the evening sunlit sky has grown dark with low rolling clouds and the rain is breaking on the streets. It's coursing in a surge again, filling the drains and gutters and the subsiding bedrock of the pavement's edge.

So, the remains of the road disappear, and all the footprints and a sense of direction: the land now a hinterland, and lost.

The boarded shops and Georgian flats are cracking and sinking down. They drop to the damp doorsteps, and the rubbish and sewage washed along in the flood, then slip with the silt to the river. And as the stone descends in a lurching, then sudden collapse, the plaster inside breaks open and reveals the wall-less rooms: the rose-patterned paper and white skirting, the delicate carved cornices and voluptuous stairways.

The rooms now empty and broken, and missing in parts, all slipping to the river and the clay, and the rainbow slick of oil.

Now life is poorer.

The radio shop is the last to fall. Maybe that much is good to know. When the roof caves in and the front gives way, the fall is strangely slow, as if almost reluctant; the grey bricks spill in a gradual defeat, brick by brick and bit by bit, slowly crushing the radios inside – the second-hand wirelesses, the Bakelites, transistors and wooden Silvertones, crushed in the slow tipping of the stone. They wash in fragments with the flood to the mud and the riverbed below.

So the future declines in this minor road that once sat by the dock, when life was richer. And so the remains of the road disappear, and all the footprints and a sense of direction: the land now a hinterland, and lost.

ACKNOWLEDGEMENTS

Matthew Bartlett, Ellie Bartlett, Carrie Blogg, Ali Enticott, Clare Greenslade, Gail McAllister, Judy Preston, Simon Preston, Kate Sutton, Rory Jay Willis, Florian Zumfelde.